# Burn

# Phone

FOR: Kim
FROM: Tom

Thomas M. Malafarina

1/04/11

# Burn Phone

FIRST SUNBURY PRESS EDITION
*Printed in the United States of America*
August 2010

**ISBN** 978-1-934597-09-5

Published by:
**Sunbury Press**
Camp Hill, PA
www.sunburypress.com

Camp Hill, Pennsylvania   USA

## Dedication

For my parents: George T. Malafarina and Lois G. Malafarina (both deceased). The things you taught me that I wanted to learn the least, have never failed to help me the most. You are always in my thoughts and in my heart.

Power tends to corrupt, and
absolute power corrupts absolutely.

John Emerich Edward Dalberg Acton,
first Baron Acton
1834 to 1902

# Chapter I

The tarnished brass customer entry-warning bell dangling above the weathered front door of the establishment clanged with a tinny clank. A large man in a glistening rain-soaked black trench coat and driving cap plodded inside, dripping what seemed like gallons of water in his wake. Ancient floorboards worn from decades of foot traffic groaned beneath his sodden leather shoes as the musty aroma of a time long since forgotten wafted up into his sinuses. The smells were like those he had experienced before in similar places of business, though he seldom had any need to frequent such places. However, these odors seemed somewhat more mildewed than those with which he had been previously familiar and much more disturbing. For a brief moment, his mind produced an image of his walking down a long flight of marble steps covered with grime and dried leaves into an underground mausoleum, housing ancient tombs of age-old rotting dead. It felt as if he were walking into a place of great decay, as if the very building, which held the store, was beginning to fester and decompose around him.

The man, Charles Wilson, appeared visibly frustrated, looking curiously from side to side as if contemplating whether the store was actually open for business or if he might be the only patron on this rainy Sunday evening. It soon became apparent he was, as there were no other customers in the large storeroom.

The dark gray paint-chipped door slammed mechanically behind him, its glass rattling loosely in its worn wooden frame, momentarily startling Wilson. He did not understand why the place made him feel so creepy, almost as if a multi-legged insect had just crawled down the back of his shirt collar, working its way down his spine, its many legs feeling feather-like against his flesh. He gave the door an unpleasant glance as if such an action might somehow help him regain his composure and shed the spine-chilling sensation. Charles looked down toward his feet, watching the raindrops drip from his coat to the floor as if in slow motion, beading up on the dust-covered floorboards before slowly seeping down into the planking to join the countless others, which had fallen during previous decades. Watching the droplets had almost a hypnotic effect on Wilson as they transformed from beaded circular orbs to flattened elliptical dots against a background of powdery sediment.

Charles lifted his head slowly as if still in a trance, beginning to study the interior of the dismal looking establishment in detail. He thought for a moment he must have been mistaken; such a place as this could never possibly have what he most desperately needed. However, he was certain the sign in the front window had advertised this store did, in fact, have what he wanted; it did sell prepaid cellular phones. The place did not seem to Wilson to be the kind of store capable of providing such a service, but he figured it couldn't hurt to ask, though it seemed like a dumb question. His mind flashed thirty years or more ago, back to a time when one of his high-school teachers had told him the only dumb question was one not asked. Wilson did not actually believe this, as he had heard many outright stupid questions asked during his lifetime.

Shaking off the remainder of the evening's rainwater, he removed his driving cap, rolling it up and putting into his right coat pocket unconsciously as he had done a thousand times before. He opened the buttons on the front of his trench coat, more out of habit than necessity. It certainly was not hot in the store; on the contrary, it almost seemed to be more damp and chillier inside the building than it had been outside in the storm.

Wilson cursed himself for leaving his own personal cell phone at home in Pennsylvania before leaving for this very important business trip. He wondered how, in the busy twenty-first century world of high technology, he could be such a fool as to leave for a business meeting two time zones across the country, without taking his cell phone - especially since the blasted thing had over a thousand business contacts stored inside. As was the case for so many of his counterparts, Wilson's cell phone had become his lifeline to the business world, providing him instant access to anyone, anytime twenty-four seven, three sixty-five.

He thought for a moment about how technology had so drastically changed his life and how he conducted business over the past ten years. He often marveled at how only what seemed like a hand full of years ago, before pagers, cell phones and such, he had managed to conduct business and run his personal life just fine. But nowadays if he was without his cell phone for even as little as an hour, Wilson felt completely cut off from the rest of the world, a world providing him with a substantial income. In addition, not a day went by when

Charles Wilson did not thank, God, Jesus and his lucky stars for that same income.

He had become aware his phone was missing as he was on the way to the Philadelphia airport, having gotten off to a late start. When the realization hit him, it was too late to turn around and go back for the phone without missing his plane. He actually considered returning home regardless and taking another flight but the next available flight was in six hours later. Since he had to get up early the next morning for a critical meeting and knew he would need a full night's sleep, he opted to not return for it. He could not believe his idiocy.

He called his wife from the airport pay phone, telling her how stupid he had been and begging her to overnight the phone to his hotel first thing Monday morning, which meant he would not likely receive it until Tuesday morning. He hated the idea of having to fork out the money for the overnight shipping, even though he could easily afford it. Wilson hated waste and in his mind, shipping the phone was simply throwing away money because of his own forgetfulness, which irked him to no end.

In the meantime, he knew he had to have some type of phone to communicate with the outside world, which of course was another waste of money. Regardless, of how he felt about it he had to acquire one, so he figured a 'burn phone' seemed like the best option. He chuckled to himself about using the term burn phone since it was the street vernacular for a prepaid cellular phone he heard used on the countless television crime shows, which he loved to watch. He wondered if maybe he was watching too many of the cop shows lately, if he was starting to insert their lingo into his normal vocabulary.

Wilson had tried to purchase a phone at the Philadelphia airport with the limited time he had available before his flight, but found all of the kiosks and shops which sold phones closed on Sunday afternoon. In addition, before he had the opportunity to investigate any further, he heard the airline announcing his flight was ready for boarding.

He assumed he would simply have to get a phone when he arrived at his destination. However, once again, fate seemed to have been working against him and none of those airport shops were open either. Luckily, he was two hours ahead of schedule thanks to the time difference. It was around 8:00 pm back in Pennsylvania but only 6:00 pm Mountain Time so he had a bit of time to look for a phone before settling down for the night.

Luckily, he had backups of all of his critical phone numbers stored on his laptop computer. While on the plane, Wilson had created a special file containing all of the numbers he would need for the next two days. He planned to print them out at the hotel's business center later so he could have them readily available.

When he arrived at his hotel he was disappointed to find the hotel gift shop closed as well, not that it mattered, as they did not carry cell phones. The front desk attendant at the hotel, a young man Wilson had thought of as a greasy post pubescent reject from Mickey D's, had pointed him to the side street around the corner from the hotel, suggesting there might be a few places still open. Unfortunately, Wilson discovered it was not so much a side street as an alley, and a dark one as well. The street was the sort of place Wilson or anyone with a shred of common sense for that matter, might do well to avoid. It was not as if Wilson was the cowardly type but, as he was often fond of saying, only a fool tempts fate. And so far, this day, fate had not done him any favors. However, tonight his need for a phone outweighed his natural tendency for precaution, so he decided a trip down the alley was his only option.

He had been wary about finding any businesses still open at 6:00 pm on Sunday evening and of course was not surprised to find all of the stores closed except for this particular one. The strange store was the first he had come to showing any potential, though he still had doubts regardless of what the window sign had advertised.

The store was markedly odd to say the least, a dark, dusty, cluttered sort of concern with an eclectic collection of bric-a-brac consisting largely of items appearing more like the sorts of things one would find in an antique store or perhaps a flea market. At first the contents of the store looked to Wilson to be typical 'junque store' nonsense and he assumed that was why the place had such an old musty odor. Upon closer examination, Wilson noted the items seemed to be much more ominous in appearance than what he had expected to find.

He noticed tattered tapestries hanging on the sidewalls starting high near the top of the fifteen-foot ceilings. The tapestries seemed to be faded and covered with cobwebs and years of dust. Dreary old oil paintings, all dark in appearance, the subjects of which he could not discern across the distance, hung askew on other walls, and leaned against stacks of grayed wooden crates piled high on the floor.

A collection of antique lamps with aged yellowed shades covered numerous paint flaked end tables. Some stood high on top of the stacks of grimy wooden crates. There was scarcely room to move about the place with only a few small winding aisles leading to the service counter near the rear of the store. There was stuff piled virtually everywhere, making the place seem more like an abandoned warehouse than an actual place of business. The longer Wilson stayed in the building, the more he realized he had made a mistake. He could not believe the stuff piled all around him.

Stuff; yes that was the best word for it, stuff. The place was overflowing with mountains of stuff. In Wilson's opinion, the store was simply a disorganized jumble. In addition, the lighting was minimal; coming from a few bare light bulbs suspended from the paint-flaked dark ceiling, and a thick layer of dust seemed to cover everything. Spider webs spanned the air between the stacked items. Wilson could not comprehend how someone would not at least take the time to clean off the webs, unless the owner of the shop was trying for some type of look for his special discerning customers. Wilson had seen store and restaurant owners go to extremes to try to produce an certain image to attract just the 'right' type of customers. He imagined a group of rich New York artsy types walking around the store, mouths agape, overcome with delight at the primitive authenticity of the place. Wilson always felt those type of people seemed to be impressed by the strangest of things. Again, he noticed how the musty smell of the place was almost overpowering. Wilson did have some minor mold and dust allergies and was glad he had at least remembered to take his medicine this morning. "What a junk shop", he thought to himself.

Wilson walked slowly down one of the narrow aisle ways; being extra cautious not to bump into anything for fear something might fall to the floor and shatter into a thousand costly pieces. "Costly indeed", he thought to himself, recalling signs he had seen in gift shops throughout his travels stating 'You Break It, You Bought It'. He was certain there was not a single thing he wanted to buy in this despicable store, that is, of course, unless they actually did have a cell phone, which was starting to seem less likely with each passing minute.

"You Break It, You Bought It" he thought to himself. His overactive imagination taking over as he looked around the store and thought to himself,

"More like, you break it and a long dead mummy ala Boris Karloff will rise up from one of those old crates, drag its bandaged leg across the store, rip your still beating heart out of your chest and eat it right before your eyes." The second of what would eventually be many such chills ran down Wilson's spine. He shook it off, blaming it on the evening's cold rain and the strangeness of the store.

As he rounded one of the aisle's curves he came upon a surprisingly shiny ceramic statue, which stood about three feet high, resting on a small dust covered table. Between the statue and the table was an old yellowed doily, once obviously ornately crafted, now filthy and torn. Upon closer examination of the statue, Wilson realized he had never seen anything quite as disturbing as this gruesome thing. It was a sculpted image of a naked male creature with an over-sized phallus jutting out from between its bowed legs; the member sculpted at full attention with the statue's right hand grasping it firmly at the base. The statue's head was arched back, eyes closed and mouth open as if howling with pleasure, sporting a Fu Manchu mustache and pointed goatee on its chin, while ram like horns protruded backward from its forehead, leading to a smooth hairless head. Looking down the length of the statue, Wilson saw the left arm of the sculpture was outstretched holding in its talon-like clawed hand, a severed head of a man with blood streaming from its eyes, its wide-open mouth and exposed stump of a neck. The dangling head appeared to be screaming as if experiencing inconceivable agony. "What was that all about?" Wilson wondered to himself. He had never seen such a horrible creation in his life.

Far up ahead, behind what he assumed to be the sales counter, Wilson noticed a slight built elderly man, probably the owner, watching his approach. The old man was definitely not dressed for business, wearing a yellowed, stained athletic tee shirt, mottled with holes; the type of shirt Wilson heard young teens refer to as 'wife beater' shirts. The old man was bald, except for a thin white ring of disheveled hair, which formed a frizzled strip about the back of the man's head connecting one huge ear to the other.

Wilson nodded a hello in the shopkeeper's direction, but the skeletal old man simply continued watching him, almost as if he had been expecting him, awaiting his arrival. He thought to himself, "This place mustn't get much business, the guy looks like he just found a long lost friend", as he continued looking around at the dingy surroundings.

Studying the setting further, Wilson could begin to distinguish some of the subject matter of the dark paintings and tapestries, and hoped he might be imagining things. The bizarre works seemed to depict scenes of unspeakable bloody violence, flailing, dismemberment, sexual orgies and other such forms of debauchery. He was suddenly thankful for the lack of lighting in the store so he might be spared some of the more shocking details of these repugnant works. A horrible sort of sick sinking feeling began to settle in his stomach. "What sort of place was this?" he wondered to himself once again.

Wilson looked again toward the service counter of the store, trying desperately to divert his eyes from the disturbing art surrounding him. He noticed a huge grandfather clock next to the service counter. The clock seemed to have a great deal or ornate carvings on its wooden frame. He initially thought for a moment he would have to remember to check the clock out when he got closer. However, after what he had seen so far, he was not certain he should. Again, he saw the old man still staring at him, a very peculiar smile appearing on his face. The cold chill returned.

Although Wilson was twice the old man's size, and probably thirty years his junior, there was something so uncomfortably odd and perhaps even threatening about the old man's demeanor, it made Wilson feel uneasy. He could not quite put his finger on it, but the feeling was certainly beginning to disturb him. A third chill descended upon him and he recalled his mother's old expression from his childhood and thought "a goose just walked across my grave." He had absolutely no idea what it meant, but that particular expression seemed to fit perfectly with how he was feeling right now, as he imagined a filthy, bloodied goose, near death, dragging itself pitifully across a grave adorned with a battered tombstone, etched with his name. He gave an involuntary shudder. Sometimes his imagination was more of a curse than a blessing.

Wilson began to think maybe he should change his plans, should simply turn and leave this strange place and perhaps with luck, find another store open further down the street. On the other hand, maybe he would just wait for his own phone to arrive Tuesday, or find another one Monday morning. Nevertheless, he really wanted to get a cell phone tonight. Perhaps he believed when he had a phone in his hands, once again, all would be right with the world. Perhaps much of the discomfort he was feeling might be simply withdrawal symptoms from not having a phone.

He tried to rationalize he was simply being ridiculous with these feelings and his apprehension was completely unfounded. Yes, this store was a bit off and the old-timer at the cash register seemed strangely out of place, but anything else he might be feeling was simply the result of a long tiring flight. "Get a grip Charlie", he scolded himself.

Wilson approached the sales counter with more than a little trepidation, as the old man waited silently, still wearing his strange expression. Now with Wilson just a few feet away he noticed, the old man was well into his seventies if not his eighties and wrinkles and age spots covered his head, arms and hands. The man's lips were thin and sunken inward as if there were few if any teeth inside the man's head to help hold their recession at bay. His large eyes were sunken into his skeletal head and dark circular bags hung beneath them. The man's ears appeared over-sized, dangling from his aged skull and Wilson could see tufts of hair sprouting from within them. The old man's nose hooked downward almost hanging over his upper lip.

Wilson heard a loud bong sound as the huge grandfather clock next to the sales counter chimed three times. It was 7:45 pm. He saw the face of the clock was an etched metal plate adorned with Roman numerals. Wilson thought he might be imagining things, but it looked like the particular font used to create the Roman numerals was actually a series of bones, one vertical bone for the 'one' numeral, a single vertical bone with a two bones forming a 'v' next to it for the 'four' numeral and so forth. The hands of the clock were shaped like a skeleton's arms with bony fingers pointing out the time. A series of finely detailed woodcarvings covered the body of the clock. As he had also suspected earlier, these carvings were equally as disturbing as everything else in the store had been; depicting scenes of sodomy, murder and virtually every sin imaginable.

Wilson turned back to the storekeeper who was still staring intently at him. Not knowing exactly what to do or say next, he simply said "Good evening" to the strange merchant.

# Chapter 2

The old man stood silently for a few seconds, wide-eyed as if transfixed in a type of hypnotic trance. Then with a degree of hesitation, he quietly replied, "Good evening." The old man's foul breath traveled the short distance across the counter causing Wilson stomach to lurch from an unspeakable stench emanating from the man. Charles was unsure if the vile odor was the result of the man's breath or his body odor or some horrible combination of both, but the repulsive scent caught him completely off guard. The sickening stench caused him to flashback to a memory from time when he was a boy of about seven.

Wilson found himself hurtled back in time, thrust into a disturbing scene from this impressionable period of his early childhood. He recalled how his aged grandfather had come to live with his family for several months. As he later discovered, his grandfather had not so much come to live with them as he had come there to die.

No one had ever actually told him the old man was dying. In fact, no one said much about what was wrong with his grandfather at all since his moving in with the Wilson family other than he was 'sick'. To a young Charlie Wilson, 'sick' meant the old man might have had a head cold, or a flu, or a perhaps stomach virus. He had no comprehension it might actually mean the man was dying. In fact, for a time after his grandfather had finally succumbed, young Charlie found himself terrified every time his mother said he, Charlie, had to go to the doctor because he was sick. After all, his grandfather had been sick and he died.

Years later, as a much older boy, Charles understood when someone in his family said one of their loved ones was 'sick', or more accurately 'really sick' it did not mean the person had a cold, flu or upset stomach, but it actually meant the person had incurable disease such as cancer. The strange thing to Charles was no one would ever speak the actual word 'cancer'. They would skirt around the edges of the disease, perhaps hoping if they did not call the illness what it really was, maybe it would somehow cease to exist. Perhaps the dread came from some unspoken superstitious fear suggesting saying the 'C-word', as it was often known, aloud might cause the speaker of the word to become 'really sick' as well. Whatever the case, even at seven years old, regardless of what everyone said he instinctively knew inside his Pap was not long for this world.

Charles remembered the fateful afternoon when his father took him by the hand and led him to the guest bedroom where his grandfather, lay unconscious, on death's door. The old man's translucent almost transparent skin sagged from his bony frame, its ashen color making the man look as though he had already been dead for a week.

Wilson recalled how there had been a horrible smell surrounding the dying man, which was almost unbearable. He remembered how as the frightened young boy he had wanted to turn and run from the moldering creature; once his beloved grandfather, but of course, he could not. Charlie knew good boys did not behave in such a manner; and he was a good boy. Therefore, with tears welling up in his eyes he stood trembling next to the dying man's bed, inhaling the nauseating stench trying desperately not to vomit, though to this day he did not know how he had managed to suppress the urge.

As a young boy, Charles had an even more overactive imagination then he did as an adult. He was an only child with few friends, a strong intellect and often spent most of his spare time watching television, reading paperback horror novels as well as amassing a huge collection of comic books. All of this fantastic input only served to fuel his already hyperactive imagination. Because of this creative mind, Charles was able to envision situations that did not exist or could never possibly occur in the real world. Moreover, he was able to do so with as much vivid detail and clarity as if he were actually watching them happen. Although this often helped to fill the young boy's empty lonely hours with fantastic imaginings, it also had a negative and dark effect, which often made its presence known at the most inappropriate of times.

As seven-year-old Charlie stood trembling next to his grandfather's deathbed staring at what would soon be and empty cadaverous shell, he started to wonder. What if? What if? He did not imagine he was a world famous physician capable of healing his grandfather. He didn't imagine he was a superhero with super healing powers to reach out and with one touch, make his grandfather well again; no not at all. Instead, as often happened, young Charlie Wilson imagined something incredibly horrible; perhaps the most horrible thing he had ever imagined in his young life.

He wondered what would happen if he found himself alone, in the room with the moldering dying creature, lying there in the foul-smelling stinking bed, the festering thing, once his beloved Pap; the pile of withered flesh and fragile bones; once vibrant, strong and full of joy having nothing but kind words for him. He wondered if he were alone with the creature, if he would see him begin to decompose right before his horrified eyes.

Then with as much clarity as if it were actually occurring, Charlie began to see it happen. First the old man's flesh began melting and sloughing off of his bones, his eyeballs sliding from their sockets, slipping down his decaying cheeks burrowing furrows in the translucent dissolving tissue, then falling onto the sweat-stained pillow below. Flies began to land on the body laying their eggs in its dark, empty eye sockets. The old man's hideous exposed skull slowly turned toward young Charlie, its fragile neck bones creaking and cracking from the strain. The Grandpa skull-thing stared through its rotten eye sockets now crawling with maggots, looked directly at Charlie, opened its black toothless maw and screamed an ear piercing death howl. From that day on Charles Wilson had the particular odor indelibly etched in his psyche, and always thought of it as the stench of death.

The unmistakable reek was what he now sensed coming from the old man behind the counter. It was as if Wilson could sense the man decaying where he stood, as if he were putrefying from the inside out. Charles understood like his grandfather, the man standing behind the counter was not long for this world. He tried to regain his composure and not show his disgust, which churned down deep inside of him, threatening to overflow in the form of a hot stream of fetid, vomit.

Wilson cleared his throat hoarsely and continued with great difficulty. "I was ...uh... surprised to see you were ... ah...open this late on a Sunday evening." Once again, the old man did not respond. He simply stood, smiling with a sunken-lip grin, staring at Wilson with almost a look of awe, as one might react when meeting a famous celebrity. The stench coming form the man was now so palpable to Wilson, he forced himself to take two steps backward to get out of range of the disgusting odor. He was certain his nasal passages were probably already so full of the reek and it would take hours of fresh air to rid himself of the foul odor. He could literally taste the death surrounding the old man. Wilson implored the man though his almost uncontrollable revulsion, "I ... I....would ... like .... to buy ...one of your..."

"..my pre-paid cellular phones." the old man interrupted in a nasal whiny voice. More of the foul stink wafted across the counter, as Wilson continued to try not to show his repulsion, his hand coming up involuntarily to shield his nose.

Then a second later, Wilson realized the man apparently knew of his reason for coming into the store, which threw him a bit off balance for a moment. How had the old man known he wanted to buy a phone? Again, Wilson felt the icy chill begin slither down his spine; snake-like. His legs were beginning to feel like rubber as if they would collapse beneath him not just from the ghastly stink flowing from the man or just from his discomfort at the old man's knowledge of the phone, but also from the strange surrealistic feeling the whole evening was beginning to acquire. This was all becoming all too bizarre, Wilson thought, as he tried to keep his increasingly foggy mind from clouding over completely.

Wilson was usually a 'fly-by-the-seat-of-his-pants' type of man who could think quickly on his feet to handle virtually any situation, which might come up, especially during one of his business exchanges. However, the drug-like feeling he was experiencing in this store was something he had never encountered and he did not quite know what to do about it.

What remained of the rational part of Wilson's mind came forward and insisted he was way off base with his apprehensiveness; surely, the old man simply must have seen him looking at the cell phone sign in the window before entering the store. Charles was in no danger from the man, whatsoever. There was no reason to let his wild imagination run away with him yet again. The man was simply a feeble old-timer who apparently missed the hygiene express for a few days, or maybe weeks, but that was all there was to it. Charles decided the sooner he finished his business and was on his way, the better.

Trying to regain his composure yet still with a slight pang of uneasiness, he replied. "Yes,...um... a pre-paid phone...." Then he continued awkwardly. "What .... what...types of phones do you carry and.... how much are they?"

"I have only one." The old man replied, while reaching underneath the sales counter.

Once again, the uneasy, almost frightening feeling overcame Wilson and for a very long upsetting moment, he had an uncontrollable premonition the old man would come up from below the counter with a version of Dirty Harry's Smith & Wesson 44 magnum and while still wearing his ridiculous grin, would blow Wilson's guts all over the store. He had no idea why he felt that way or why the sensation was so overpowering. He became aware of a bead of sweat forming above his lip, as he involuntarily tensed up, the muscles in his arms and neck becoming almost rigid. The hair prickled on the back of his neck as his upper lip was now glistening with sweat. He wondered what, in the name of God was wrong with him. The old man was obviously harmless. Wilson could not understand why he was experiencing so much anxiety.

"Do you only have one type of phone?" Wilson inquired apprehensively; more to calm himself than anything. He was simply trying to make conversation to help put his fears at ease. As the old man slowly lifted his hand from below the counter, Wilson knew this would be the decisive moment. The moment when the old timer would point the barrel of the massive weapon at Wilson and within two seconds, would splatter his guts like raw hamburger, all over the piles of junk stacked throughout the place. He figured afterward the old guy wouldn't even have the decency to clean up the mess, since cleanliness obviously was not his strong suit.

Then Wilson imagined the old man releasing a pack of wild starving hounds from the basement of the store. The beasts would swarm his dead carcass, systematically devouring his remains, picking his bones clean, leaving no trace he was ever in the store, other than his skeleton, which the old guy would probably hang from a pole and sell to some medical college or something. He thought to himself, "Charlie, you have to do something about that imagination of yours." He recalled how often had he heard his parents say those very words to him as a young child.

"No...One phone." The old man replied, returning his hand to the counter top and waking Wilson from his nightmarish vision. Charles was relieved to see the storekeeper did not have a gun ready to blow his head off, but instead the old man had set an odd-looking cell phone on the counter top.

Odd looking was an understatement. The phone was about two inches wide and about four inches tall, blood red, with a row of gaudy sequins encircling the outside edge of the body. It appeared to contain only numeric keys from one to nine and a simple viewing screen. Upon closer examination; Wilson saw the numeric buttons were over-sized chrome keys shaped like skulls, complete with red eyes and black nose sockets. It had no '0' key, no send button, just nine numbers with nine ridiculous chrome skull buttons. It looked like something a teenage Goth wanna-be might purchase, or would more likely, shoplift.

The appearance of the phone was appalling to Wilson. It would never do. How could he walk into a business meeting sporting that hideous phone? For a moment, he forgot all about his misgivings concerning the old man and spoke his mind.

"Don't you have anything else, perhaps more business-like in appearance?" Wilson inquired.

The old man continued to stare at Wilson, his smile of fascination slowly changing to a slight frown of disappointment. Wilson felt the strange sensation crawling back into his stomach. He was starting to think perhaps speaking so candidly to this old man might not have been the best idea. The old man held out a hand offering the phone to Wilson, who noticed the filthy condition of the man's fingers. They were black with grime and Wilson could see the underside of the man's long yellowed chipped fingernails. He did not wish to be rude but knew there was no way he planned to take anything from the man's grubby paw. The old man slowly said, "this one phone is all I have.... and it is meant for you."

Wilson wondered what the man was implying, saying the phone was meant for him. It seemed like a very odd thing to say. Between the strange store, the old man's comments, Wilson's imagination and his gut sounding warning alarms, everything seemed to be going south in a hurry. The man's demeanor from the start had been as if he was waiting, was expecting Wilson to arrive. However, how could that possibly be? Wilson understood why he was feeling apprehensive and why his imagination was running away with him, this old man was just plain spooky.

He decided perhaps the best way to proceed for now was to just try to ignore the old man's mysterious comment. He decided to ask another question, one relating to the functionality of the phone, hoping to deflect what was appearing to be an escalating confrontation, "Well ...um...how many minutes does it have preloaded?"

The old man just stared at him as if he hadn't heard. Wilson continued, "You know, how .... How many minutes will I get on this phone?.... How long can I use it?"

"It has whatever you will need," the old storekeeper said cryptically, continuing to stare at Wilson, with a far away expression.

Again, Wilson found himself perplexed by the store owner's enigmatic reply. His original fears were subsiding and now he was becoming just plain annoyed with the entire situation. He thought to himself with frustration, "Can't this old coot answer a simple question in English? What is it with all the mysterious responses?"

He realized he was in no real position to debate with the shopkeeper and knew the sooner he wrapped up this transaction the better. He needed a phone and if this was all the storekeeper had then he had to either take it or leave it. He said aloud in frustration more to himself than to the store owner, "Well, I guess it's my own damned fault for forgetting my phone..."

"Damned indeed." The old man interjected. Now the eerie grin had returned to his wrinkled face. Wilson realized not only did the storekeeper have the upper hand, but also the old man knew it, and was enjoying it immensely. Wilson looked into the old man's eyes and for a moment was once again reminded of his childhood experience with his dying grandfather and the imagined grinning skull opening its mouth to howl its cry of death. Wilson would not have been surprised to see this old man shriek the very death howl right now. Wilson felt the chill return and begin creeping down his spine as he looked at the disturbing smiling face of the ancient merchant.

Wilson tried to work around the lump in his throat and continued uncomfortably, "Um... well... how much is it?"

The old man, said, "Do you really feel you are in a position to negotiate price?" The directness of his reply surprised Wilson, catching him off guard.

"L...l....look," Wilson stammered, "I need the phone, alright?  I just don't like the idea of you trying to take advantage of me."

The old man smiled a full smile revealing a cavernous mouth with only two or three rotten teeth remaining. "Spoken like a true businessman." The old man replied, "However, I have no intention of taking advantage of you, Mr. Wilson. As I said, this phone is meant for you."

The statement stopped Wilson in his tracks. He thought to himself, "I never met this old goat before in my life. In fact, I have never been in this part of this city before. How did he know my name?"

# Chapter 3

Wilson stood silently for a moment, unable to speak, looking at the man with uncertainty and confusion. "Excuse ...me..." Wilson said uncomfortably, "I don't recall telling you my name."

The inexplicable elderly man behind the counter wore a smug expression of confidence as Wilson understood with frustration, that the man was continuing to play his sick psychological game.

"You didn't." The old man said, still wearing his strange look, "But nonetheless, I know you are Charles Wilson, a businessman from Pennsylvania, and you need this phone." He handed the phone out to Wilson.

Wilson did not even look at the phone. As if in a trance, without realizing what he was doing, he reached out his hand, took the phone from the man and tucked it into his left trench coat pocket. The old man appeared satisfied, and Wilson had absolutely no idea he had even accepted the phone.

The old man finally said, "The phone is yours and you must now pay the nonnegotiable price for it."

Wilson stammered angrily, "All right. I've played this game a thousand times before, so let's get to it. What is your asking price?"

"Ah yes." The old man continued, once again reaching under the counter. When his hand returned, it held a menacing looking large caliber handgun.

It was exactly what Wilson had feared earlier, the crazy old codger was going to blow a hole in him the size of Rhode Island. He started to step back, when to his surprise, the old man turned the gun around, placing his wrinkled hand on the barrel and directing the handle toward Wilson.

Wilson stammered, "I .. I don't want ...your damned gun. I just want to .. pay for that ridiculous phone you have for sale and then get out of here."

The old man continued to hold the gun by the barrel, the weight causing it to quiver slightly in his weakening grasp, "All in good time Mr. Wilson. As I said, a price must be paid." Wilson was becoming more confused by the minute. How much more outlandish could this situation get? "The price for the phone is one death." The old man said. "Mine. You must take my life in order to pay the required price for the phone. It has been preordained, and thus it must be so."

Wilson's mouth dropped in disbelief. "Take his life? Preordained?" He thought, "Surely, this man must be insane." Then Charles barked, "Old man, you must be out of your damned mind. I have never killed anyone or anything in my entire life. I don't even own a gun and I have no reason to want to bring any harm to you. You must be some kind of crazy old suicidal fool or something. I am out of here." Wilson said while starting to turn to leave, only to find suddenly he could no longer move.

He wondered fearfully what was happening to him. Literally, every muscle in his body became paralyzed. Panic seized Wilson and a cold sweat began to stream from every pore in his motionless body.

The old man continued to stand holding the huge handgun by its quaking barrel. "Mr. Wilson," the old man continued, "You may like to believe you have never killed anyone in your life but it is not necessarily so. Does the name James O'Connell mean anything to you?"

Wilson stood stock still unable to move or speak as the old man continued. "Yes, I can see you do recognize his name. You are probably thinking you had nothing to do with his death, as it was a suicide. You might say the same thing about Michael Johnson, Norman Gladstone and William Dawson. Is that not true? All of these were likewise suicides. Each of these men took his own life. You could always argue you did not kill them, but the fact of the matter is you did."

"Your harsh business dealings with these gentlemen resulted in very successful deals for you and your company but not so good for them. As a direct result of your actions, these men lost their businesses and their property, their lives were ruined, their families abandoned them and eventually they took their own lives. And since suicide is a mortal sin, these gentlemen are now all enjoying an eternity of torture in the deepest regions of Hell."

"But I digress. Speaking of business, I have important business with my master on the other side, and you must help me to get to him. Only you can assist me in crossing over. I can only accomplish this very important task if a certain set of criteria are met and you, my friend, are a very important element in my meeting those criteria."

Not in control of his own movements, Wilson looked down and saw his right arm reaching out and taking hold of the handle of the gun as the old man released his grip of the barrel. Wilson found himself with his right arm outstretched grasping the trigger of the huge weapon. He tried to release the gun, but could not. Somehow, the old man was manipulating him like a mindless puppet, causing him to point the gun directly at the man's head.

"Very good, Mr. Wilson. However, you see, I unfortunately can only control you to a point. It is very important; in fact, it is mandatory, you pull the trigger on your own. I cannot do it for you. You must kill me willingly of your own volition." The old man explained. "So if you would be so kind as to just go ahead and pull the trigger, you will be free to leave and be on your way. It should not be a great challenge for a man such as yourself. As I have pointed out, you have already been responsible for killing many men, perhaps not directly and not this up close and personal, but nonetheless you were just as responsible as if you had pulled the trigger yourself. What is one more death on an already tainted soul like yours?"

Wilson tried again to speak and discovered doing so took all of his strength. Even with all of his willpower, he could scarcely utter a few simple words. "I won't..... do it.....I .. can't ... do it." Wilson realized he might be in a standoff for a very long time with this crazy old man, as there was no way he would ever willingly pull the trigger.

The old man stood, watching patiently in silence. The store was completely quite now and seemed frozen in time. Wilson could hear the floor creak slightly beneath the old man's feet as he shifted his weight from foot to foot. He could hear the ticking of the huge grandfather clock, which now seemed more like a pounding of a drum in his brain. After a few more tense minutes, Charles could tell it had become apparent to the old man he would not pull the trigger.

"I see." The old man replied, "I didn't suspect you had what it took to just shoot me in cold blood, your methods for killing seem to be more passive than aggressive. You apparently like to drive people to kill themselves rather than have the courage to do the actual deed yourself. I had hoped you might have what it took, but to be honest, few people do. I know you are a fan of television, but it is a lot different in the flesh, so to speak. Don't feel so badly about it, Mr. Wilson."

"Perhaps there is something I can do to motivate you a bit. As I said, the price for the phone is my death. However, if you refuse to kill me, as I require than I suppose I will just have to kill you. The fact is, Charles, one of us is going to die within the next few minutes and I strongly suspect you will not want it to be you. So I must insist you reconsider your options."

Wilson stood like a statue, the gun trained on the old man's head. He noticed the only movement he could manage was in his index finger. He tried to keep his finger from getting a spasm or twitch and accidentally applying any unwanted pressure to the trigger. However, the more he tried to prevent it the more he feared it might actually happen. Perhaps the trigger of the gun was very sensitive and the thing might go off despite his efforts to prevent it from doing so.

Then a terrifying thing happened. The old man behind the counter began to tremble from head to toe as his face reddened and beads of sweat formed on his wrinkled brow. His eyes stared at Wilson and seemed to be bulging from their sockets as he now shook violently. Wilson could hear the floorboards begin to rattle under the man's quaking body. The man's hands rested on the service counter, which began to shake with such ferocity

Wilson was certain it would shatter to pieces at any moment.

From his frozen position Wilson could see the storekeeper was changing, transforming before his eyes. The man arched and twisted as if stretching his back and neck muscles. His hands left the counter, as his arms seemed to move inward toward the centerline of his body while the tremors increased in their savagery. The man closed his bulging eyes leaning his head backward in a fashion very similar to that of the wretched demon statue Wilson had seen earlier.

At the front of the man's forehead, Wilson noticed two bumps begin to protrude and stretch the skin to the breaking point. The skin ripped open splattering Wilson's face with small speckles of blood as a pair of horns began to emerge from the torn flesh, growing rapidly longer, glistening with the man's blood, curling up like those of a ram. Wilson again remembered the horrible sculpture and could not comprehend how this could possibly be happening.

The air filled with a horrible stench the likes of which Wilson had never encountered; a combination of sulfur, human waste, dead animals, rotten meat and God only knew what else. He felt the urge to vomit even more so than when he had smelled the man's disgusting body odor earlier. The old man's mouth hung agape. Wilson noticed the man's few remaining tombstone teeth were falling out and clattering onto the counter top, bloody filaments dangling from their blackened roots. Inside the man's foul cavern of a mouth, Wilson saw long sharp fangs, rising like stalagmites out from the man's puss-filled bleeding gums, replaced these missing teeth.

Wilson noticed a pointed goatee and mustache had appeared on the old man face. He wondered why he hadn't noticed it before. Was it always there, or did it just appear? He was not certain. The changing old man drooled maggots from between his fangs. The worms slid downward on a steady stream of blood and slobber congealing in his demonic beard.

The old man's hands had become much larger growing huge razor-like talons. His arms now reached high into the air, no longer aged and scrawny but massive and undulating with rope-like muscles, drenched with glistening sweat. To Wilson, it appeared as if the man was now close to seven feet tall. He also realized his own arm had been raised allowing the barrel of the gun to remain trained on the hideous creatures head.

In a low guttural voice barely able to articulate human speech, the creature before him said "Mr. Wilson, ...one of us is going to die here tonight and I honestly don't believe you want it to be you...." The beast raised its incredible clawed hands to strike down and slash Wilson to shreds.

Without taking the time to think, simply reacting, Wilson's finger twitched on the trigger of the handgun, which exploded with a tremendous force, knocking Charles backward to the floor. He lay there for a moment dazed and deafened by the blast. He was unsure if the demon had struck him or if the recoil of the gun had knocked him down. Likewise, he was not certain if his shot had actually hit the creature or not. He had no idea what happened to the gun as it was no longer in his grasp.

Slowly, as he regained some of his orientation, he was able to roll over onto his side and get up on his knees, resting on his sweating, trembling palms. His mind seemed to be spinning out of control and it took a few moments for him to regain his equilibrium. Then staggering clumsily to his feet, ears still ringing, Wilson stumbled to the sales counter, grabbing it for support, while trying to determine what had become of the horrid nightmare creature. He took a few apprehensive steps around the counter; certain he might either collapse to the floor, wary that the beast behind the counter would arise again and rip him to pieces. He thought strangely of how just a few moments ago he had wanted nothing to do with the man's handgun and now he wished nothing else but to have it in his hands. However, it could not be seen anywhere.

To his astonishment, as he looked cautiously over the top of the counter, he did not see the demonic creature, but instead saw a frail old man lying dead on the floor in a pool of blood, his brains and skull fragments splattered high on the wall behind the counter dripping downward in gray and crimson streams.

"What the Hell!" Wilson said "The creature, the monster, where is the monster?"

Wilson was aghast. He knew the old man had transformed. He saw it with his own eyes. He knew he had been just seconds away from a horrible death at the hands of the enormous demon thing, yet now it was gone. All that remained was the dead body of a helpless broken old man. Then Wilson came to a frightening realization, "Sweet God in Heaven. I know I saw a beast.. but... but ... where is .. the... the monster. Did I really kill ... this old man in cold blood?" The grandfather clock next to the counter bonged eight times echoing through the vacant store, seeming to do so almost as loudly as the blast of the handgun.

With that, Wilson spun around staggering from side to side trying desperately to weave his way back to the front door, to escape this nightmarish place. As he moved jerkily through the store it appeared to him as if the air around him was changing. He felt the meager light in the room diminishing even further and thought he heard buzzing, like an incredible swarm of angry hornets were behind him, pursuing him.

As he hurried clumsily down the aisle, he bumped into the demonic ceramic statue causing it to topple to the floor where it shattered into hundreds of pieces. Looking down at the remains of the statue, Wilson saw thousands of worms and maggots crawling among the broken shards as if they had infested and filled the inside of the thing. His breath caught in his throat. He stumbled to the front door and finally mustered the courage to turn and look back just before making his exit. He could not believe what he saw.

The place seemed to be disintegrating before his very eyes. It was as if he was looking at a picture in a book and thousands of insects were devouring the picture from the center outward. As the world he thought he was part of was being eaten, all that remained in the center was a spreading blackness, darker than anything he had ever seen.

The entire contents of what was once a much-cluttered store was disappearing as the insect things continued munching away at reality. Approximately five feet in front of Wilson the room was as the store originally looked but beyond that was nothingness. Wilson grabbed the handle of the door, flung it open and headed out onto the empty sidewalk, slamming the door behind him. He stopped for a moment and looked in the front window not seeing any of the signs advertising prepaid cellular phones which had previously been there.

He placed his hands on the window and tried to look into the store, seeing only blackness. His hands felt a vibration as thousands of the insect things he heard in the store banged against the glass of the front window. He could not see them in the darkness, but he could feel their tiny bodies slamming against the glass. Wilson shivered from head to toe, backing away from the window, dazed as if in a horrible nightmare.

Charles was confused beyond all comprehension. What had just happened to him? For that matter, had anything actually happened to him? Did he just have some sort of bizarre hallucination? Had he actually even entered the store, or had he fallen into some sort of seizure outside of the obviously abandoned building and imagine the whole thing? Nothing made sense to him anymore. He could no longer recall what was real and what he may have imagined.

He staggered backward away from the storefront, stumbled off the pavement onto the dark, rainy side street, almost losing his footing. He began tripping back clumsily toward his hotel, dazed and bewildered. Then he stopped dead in the middle of the abandoned alleyway realizing something; his ears were still ringing. They had been fine when he left the hotel, but they were ringing as if from the result of a loud explosion. If he never entered the store, if there was no old man, if there was no demon and if he hadn't fired the gun taking the old man's life, then why were his ears ringing?

Wilson's stomach lurched with the sinking feeling perhaps all of the events of the past few minutes actually may have happened. He felt the urge to vomit, and did not even care to suppress it; as perhaps vomiting would purge his body and soul from all of the horrible thoughts swarming through his mind. Then, just as quickly, his stomach settled and the urge passed.

Wilson stood still in the middle of the street trying to comprehend what had or had not happened to him; what was real and what was imagined. Unconsciously, he reached his left hand into the pocket of his trench coat and felt something inside. It felt like a cell phone.

## Chapter 4

One touch of the cell phone in his pocket and the realization of the implications surrounding the atrocious phone once again sent a chill down Wilson's spine. He could not recall the old man handing him the phone and did not recall putting it into his coat pocket, but he obviously must have done so. That meant the old man had to have actually existed and the incident at the store must have actually occurred.

Wilson's brain started to play a back and forth game of illogical logic. He did not understand how he could have ended up with the phone if none of the events of the past hour had actually happened. Yet, since he did have the phone then surely everything must have happened as he now recalled. Moreover, how could something so bizarre have possibly happened? Yet, if it all had somehow taken place, then why and how was the mysterious store, now abandoned? However, if it had not happened, why did he have the cell phone?

Wilson pondered this confusing paradox for a few moments longer, then decided he had better let it go lest it might drive him insane. Slowly and with much trepidation, he pulled the phone from his pocket to examine it under the dim streetlight. The silver skull shaped numeric keys shined against the background of the blood red phone cover. The phone seemed to produce an almost tactile vibration in his hand, or perhaps a pulse might be more accurate. It made him feel sick inside to feel this phone, as if it were some vile disgusting living thing he held in his hand, its cover feeling less like plastic and more like mottled flesh. He wanted to throw the phone away in revulsion, but could not seem to will himself to do so. Charles simply could not get his mind around what may have or may not have happened on this terrible evening. He stood in the dwindling rain as if in a trance, hair now drenched with rainwater, staring down at the hideous phone.

"It's not a very smart idea being alone on a dark street on a night like this." A voice spoke from the drizzly darkness directly behind Wilson. He turned around slowly to try to see the source of the voice and in the shadows could make out a large menacing figure. A hefty man dressed in a leather jacket, black watch cap, and jeans over dark leather boots stood watching Wilson, his face obscured in shadows. The man appeared to be about six feet three inches and about two hundred and fifty solid pounds. As if through some primal instinct buried deep in his genes, Wilson understood this man was not approaching as a friend. He felt the hairs on the back of his neck stand on end.

Although Wilson was a big man perhaps equal in height to the mysterious stranger, he was not in the apparent superior shape the man obviously was and therefore assumed trying to physically confront the man or even attempt to run away would be a very bad idea. Wilson did not know what to do or say, so he simply stood with the ridiculous newly acquired cell phone grasped tightly in his left hand.

"What do you have for me?" the sinister figure inquired from the shadows.

For a brief moment of confusion, Wilson thought perhaps the man was asking for the strange phone, and actually thought about holding it out to him. Although the idea seemed somewhat odd to Wilson, it was no more peculiar than any other events occurring on this bizarre night. Charles was beginning to feel as if he might actually be dreaming all of this. He imagined for a moment in reality, he might be at home in a coma, being the victim of some sort of stroke or something of that nature, and all of these occurrences might actually be the result of a bad hallucination.

Wilson stammered to the man. "I don't think I have... anything for you, I don't know... I am not sure... what you want."

The man replied in a condescending tone, "That's not a real tough one, Einstein. How's about we start with your wallet. How's about you give me your wallet and we'll see what transpires from there."

It finally registered with Wilson the man was not part of the strange happenings of this eventful evening, but was simply a robber, a mugger, a common hood hiding there in the shadows with a single intent; to take his money. Wilson found himself strangely relieved the thug was just what he appeared to be, and the man would not suddenly morph into some sort of demon or unnatural creature. The man was human, nothing more. Compared to what he believed he had been through earlier in the evening Wilson felt no fear whatsoever. He knew how to deal with people and this character was just that; a person, nothing more. He had spent a lifetime making deals and arbitrating negations and this would simply be another deal.

"Look." Wilson suggested, "My wallet is of no use to you, neither are my credit cards. I have over three hundred dollars in cash in my wallet. You can have it, no strings attached. Please just let me keep my cards so I can get back home."

With that, the stranger produced something from his pocket, which flipped open to reveal a large knife blade. "Look, friend. Maybe you do not quite comprehend the gravity of your situation. I am not what you might call your typical mugger. I am someone of shall we say a much higher intellect than your traditional street-thug. I carefully pick and study my subjects and am extremely careful about with which of those aforementioned subjects I choose to do my business. I am very good and what I do and take great pride in my work, so allow me to explain the rules of my trade to you in order that we can remove all confusion. See, you don't get to tell me what I can and can't have. I, being the individual holding this razor sharp implement capable of rendering death and mayhem, get to tell you, the unarmed cowering victim, what you will or will not give me. Got that? Very well. Now be so kind as to give me your wallet... and give it to me now or else you are unfortunately going to end up lying in this wet stinking alley watching your own blood and guts run down the sewer until you slowly and painfully die. How is that for a clear and concise explanation?"

Wilson realized the man standing before him was not some hyped up junkie or stupid criminal. The man was frighteningly articulate, which momentarily made Wilson wonder what convergence of unfortunate events could occur to take someone such as this man and turn him from a potential scholar to a common robber. Perhaps the man was simply one of those mentally bent or broken people who, although intelligent, ended up gravitating to the world of crime. With that in mind, Wilson decided it might be best for him to cut his losses and give the man what he wanted; but he would not do so without trying some type of defensive counter measure.

Wilson remembered the phone in his left hand and decided the perhaps he could distract the man long enough to dial 911. Then surely, the operator would hear what was going on and perhaps could triangulate his signal or track his phone using GPS as he had seen them do on his favorite television cop shows. Perhaps the operator would hear enough to discern what was transpiring and would send help. Either way, he had to try something.

He said to his attacker, "OK. I understand what you are saying and I will not try to stop you. Please just don't hurt me. See, I am reaching into my back pocket to get my wallet. I will go nice and slowly, OK?"

"Use two fingers, my friend... and please don't even think about doing anything stupid," The robber reminded. The man watched him with hawk-like eyes ready for the slightest wrong move. With the thug just a few feet away from him, face still hidden in shadows, Wilson knew any attempt at counter attack on his part would prove futile and probably fatal. He was sure the attacker would not hesitate to gut him as he had promised.

Although cautious and fearful of his attacker, Wilson found a hatred for the man boiling up inside of him. He had never known he could feel such utter loathing for another human being. However, no one had ever made him feel so useless, so helpless and violated as this man had. He understood in the deepest and darkest recesses of his soul if he got the upper hand on this criminal, he would not hesitate to slice the man from stem to stern; happily watching his entrails fall from his body and slither down the sewer drain like so much refuse.

As he started to reach into his right back pocket to get his wallet, keeping the robber's eyes trained on that activity, he used his left hand, which was now down along his side to press what he hoped was the 'nine' key on the cell phone. He squeezed the button surreptitiously yet angrily as if letting all of his fury flow into that single act.

Wilson, felt something move eerily just under the flesh-like skin of the phone, and imagined the motion of a parasitic worm as it burrowed and slithered just under the outermost layer of his own flesh. Once again, he felt like throwing the phone as far away as possible, but he knew it might be his only hope for reaching help.

"Lets move it genius, I don't have all night," the robber demanded.

Wilson slowly removed his wallet from his right pants pocket with two fingers and started to move it into view swinging a long and slow arc to his right, while simultaneously attempting to feel for what he hoped would be the 'one' numeric key on the cell phone. However, before he had the opportunity to press the second button, he heard what sounded like a violent ripping sound coming from behind his would-be assailant.

# Chapter 5

The large mugger heard the sound as well, and while keeping the knife trained on Wilson, he turned slightly trying with peripheral vision to look behind him with the hopes of seeing what had made the strange noise. What he saw made him forget completely about Wilson and his wallet, because what was happening defied anything any sane person could ever hope to comprehend.

From a point about nine feet above the street stretching downward to the ground, a large rip seemed to have formed in the world. It was as if someone was showing a full size movie of the view looking back down the alley and using a scorching blade to cut a large rip down the center of the screen. The rip was about a foot wide in the middle, black as pitch inside, and tapered off to nothing at the top and bottom. The edges of the slash were glowing with white-hot embers like molten steel in a boiling cauldron. The most peculiar thing about it was Wilson could see cars moving about on the main street far down the alley behind the huge black rip, oblivious to what was happening on this dark side street. It was as if a gash had opened in the very fabric of reality.

"What the hell," the robber shouted in bewilderment.

Wilson was likewise staring in astonishment. He was so shocked he had forgotten completely about dialing for help and simply stood transfixed with his wallet in his right hand suspended by two trembling fingers, and the strange cell phone in his left. Then he noticed a foul and familiar unpleasant odor. He had smelled the same nauseating stench inside the mysterious store emanating from the old man.

Wilson watched the mugger look back and forth between him and the unearthly split in the world as if trying to determine which posed the biggest threat, but Wilson instinctively understood where the real danger came from. He heard distant moaning, howling and screaming coming from deep inside the giant wound in the world as if hundreds of thousands of creatures were simultaneously crying out in pain, and Wilson knew the thug was in more trouble than the unfortunate soul could have ever imagined.

From behind the robber, Wilson heard a scraping sound as from the bottom of the dark slit, several long slime covered tentacles began to emerge and flop about the street as if blindly searching for something. Their texture and color appeared to be almost reptilian; or perhaps some human/reptile hybrid with slimy greens blended with flesh tones and browns. As the tentacles groped along the wet street, steam rose in plumes from their apparently flaming hot flesh, which simultaneously evaporated the puddles of rainwater.

Wilson noticed the ends of the tentacles were sprouting miniature human-like hands with long gleaming claws. Before the robber had time to react, several of the hand/tentacles grabbed him around his ankles pulling quickly, knocking the man off balance, landing him sharply on his back, splashing water droplets upward to join the growing plumes of forming steam. The once deadly blade flew from his hand and clattered harmlessly to the street. The thug screamed in pain as the incredible hand/tentacles burned away his pant legs melting the flesh off of his ankles, instantly cauterizing the man's wounds, stopping blood flow. Then grasping firmly on the now exposed anklebones, the tentacles began to pull.

In the distance beyond the night-black gash, Wilson could see people walking along the pavement completely oblivious to the ear-splitting screaming coming from the downed man as he struggled in vain to free himself from the torturous grasp. It was as if the horrors occurring in the alley were happening a million miles away in some unknown dimension and no one was aware of them.

Slowly the tentacles began to withdraw backward into the white-hot crevice, pulling the screaming, kicking robber along with them. As the man's body got closer to the opening, Wilson heard the screaming and howling from within the darkness opening getting even louder and more chaotic. He imagined thousands of demons, or whatever it was waiting just beyond the unearthly portal, celebrating the man's capture and anticipating his arrival with a hunger beyond satisfaction.

The scorching fingers began dragging the wailing thief into the slit, but his body was much too large to fit. As he was dragged forcibly through the opening, the glowing white-hot sides of the fracture began to blaze even brighter. The man's clothing burned instantly and the outer layers of his flesh peeled away from his bones, exposing hipbones then the sides of his rib cage; all of his flesh vaporizing, his blood steaming away to a sickening pink mist, as he was dragged howling into the void.

The entire process reminded Wilson of a laser surgery show he had watched on one of the educational channels. As chunks of skin separated, severed from the man's body, some fell to the street. As if on queue, small flesh-covered eyeless worm-like creatures slithered out of the opening heading directly toward the flesh as if guided by the burning aroma. They clutched the flesh chunks in their mouths, filled with thousands of needle-like teeth, and began dragging the remnants back into the hole. Steam rose from the surface of their writhing bodies as the rain splashed down on them. The dying man screamed and begged for mercy as his flayed body disappeared into the blackness.

Wilson continued to stare helplessly at the horrors unfolding before him. Then as mysteriously as it had appeared, the burning sides of the opening began to move closer together, fusing as Wilson watched the alley before him return to normal. Before the opening had completely sealed, Wilson heard a voice in his mind sounding like the horrible old man from the store saying, "Well done, my good and faithful servant."

Although Wilson had not been a regular at church of late, he had attended enough Sunday school in his youth to recognize it as an expression from the bible. "Well done my good and faithful servant," he repeated to himself. He also knew however, the bible, Jesus, God or Heaven had nothing whatsoever to do with the unholy events of this evening. Something purely evil was behind what had just unfolded before his astonished eyes.

Dumbfounded, Wilson slowly staggered toward the spot where the rip had occurred and with his right hand still holding his wallet, tried to reach out to find the former chasm in the world, only to feel nothing but the cool rainy night air. There was not a single sign of any blood or bits of flesh mixed with the rain puddles on the ground. The worm-like creatures must have collected everything remaining of his unknown assailant. He did however see the attacker's switchblade lying on the ground glistening in the moonlight.

For a moment, the world seemed to fade in and out and Wilson thought perhaps he might pass out, go insane or both. He bent down and placed his hands on his knees to allow blood to flow back to his head. He then noticed he still had the wallet in his right hand, and slowly returned it to his back pocket. He took several deep breaths, and then unable to control himself any longer, he vomited.

Once finished, standing carefully, wiping the vomit residue from his lips with the sleeve of his left arm Wilson saw the red cell phone still clutched tightly in his hand. He thought to himself, "Did this ghastly cell phone cause all of this to happen?" Wilson deliberated for a moment about finding a dumpster or sewer opening and throwing the accursed phone away. But, somehow, he knew deep inside this futile action would do no good. He knew no matter what he did to this phone, whenever he reached his hand into his coat pocket, it would somehow always be there. Even if he succeeded in smashing the phone into a thousand pieces and discarded each individual part at completely different locations, he understood the phone would return. He did not know how he knew this but he instinctively did. The old man in the store had said the phone was 'meant' for him.

Wilson did the only thing he could think of and tucked the phone back into his trench coat pocket, bent down and picked up the dead robber's switchblade, returned the blade to its closed position and tucked it into his right pocket. He did not ever intend to press even one of the buttons on the cell phone again for as long as he lived. Unfortunately, somehow Wilson also knew this would not be true, no matter how much he wanted it to be. Because there was a strange, almost magnetic attraction with this phone he knew would return to tempt him, would lure him back, would slowly try to change him. Maybe it would try to tap into the darker side of Wilson he believed existed in every human; an ancient and primal survival side of him. He understood there was a power within the phone, which could possibly prove very useful to a man with the cunning business sense of someone like himself. Although on the surface he wanted to deny any attraction and think only of the revulsion he felt for the phone, deep inside his subconscious accepted and acknowledged the attraction.

Like the reformed junkie who never got over the need for an elusive next fix, Wilson somehow needed to learn more about this phone, the attraction was too great, too incredible. What this all meant and why he had been thrust in the middle of the situation he did not yet understand, but believed he would find out very soon.

## Chapter 6

Charles Wilson sat nervously on the edge of his bed staring across the room at the strange cell phone lying on the hotel dresser, a glass of half consumed whiskey from the mini bar in his hand. Upon returning to his room, he had poured himself a glass of Seagram's' Crown Royal to calm his nerves, downed it in one gulp then poured himself another. He had been trying to find a way to relax, to stop his voice from quivering and to stop his hands from shaking. He needed to call his wife to let her know he arrived and knew she would notice the anxiety in his voice instantly, so he had to try to find a way to keep her from sensing something was wrong; which of course, there most certainly was.

Once he had finished his second drink and started on a third, Charles felt perhaps he was comfortable enough to talk. He called, using the hotel room phone; keeping his eye trained on the 'other phone'. In addition to reminding her about shipping his cell phone, he had an overpowering premonition he should make sure everything was all right at home. After what he had been through tonight, at least after what he believed he had been through, learning nothing was wrong at home would go a long way to making him feel much better.

His wife, Sarah, answered the phone and he did is best to sound as normal as possible. However, knowing him as well as she did, she immediately sensed something was wrong. "Charlie, are you all right? You don't sound like yourself."

"Yes, Honey I'm fine." He lied with as much conviction as he could muster. "I am just a bit tired from the trip. But, for the most part I am getting along without it pretty well, even without my phone. It is just a small adjustment for me, is all. Besides, I am sure you will remember to send it to me tomorrow morning."

"Don't worry, Charlie." She replied. "I won't forget about it. If I stop at the store, first thing tomorrow morning, you should be receiving it at the hotel by 10:00 am Tuesday morning. Speaking of your cell phone, did you ever get around to picking up a burn phone?"

For a moment, Charles was silent, not knowing quite how to respond; the question and the use of the term 'burn phone' catching him off guard. The phrase now had a whole new meaning than it did before. "Burn phone." He thought to himself. "Burning fires of Hell phone." The very thought of that horrific phone and what it had done earlier to the man in the alley caused him to break out in a cold nervous sweat. "N...No" He lied again, with what he hoped sounded like sincerity, but which he didn't believe sounded sincere at all. "No... I couldn't get one, No stores were open ... so... I .. I.. figured... I would just wait and maybe try again tomorrow or else I may simply wait until Tuesday morning.. you know... when my real phone gets here."

"You've got to be kidding me. You, surviving without a cell phone in your hand until Tuesday morning? I don't think that is possible. It might be easier for you to survive without food or oxygen."

She teased. "But not without your cell phone. Honey, you even brought that stupid cell phone of yours on vacation last year, for God's sake."

"Maybe so." He said carefully trying to avoid the real issue, "But ... believe it or not well...I am kind of enjoying being out of touch from the rest of the world for a while. I might find it to be a nice change." All the while he was speaking with Sarah, his eyes never left the blood red phone sitting ominously across the room. "If you have an emergency, you have my number here at the hotel, and here is the number at the office of the client where I have a meeting tomorrow morning." He waited for her to get a pencil and paper then gave her the number.

"I was thinking it might actually be nice to slow down a bit and do things the way we used to do them. You know, 'old school', as they say." He had no idea if what he had just said sounded convincing to his wife or not, but it sounded like an incredible mountain of garbage to his own ears.

"Yeah right Charlie. I believe you." She replied sarcastically, "I'll give you till noon tomorrow. If you can hold out that long, I will be amazed. And, if you can somehow last until Tuesday morning when your phone arrives, then the next time we go on vacation, that cell phone of yours stays home. Understand?"

"Yes I understand." Wilson said surrendering, "It's a deal." Then Wilson thought about the old man in the store, recalling how the man had said the phone was 'meant for' him. He also thought about how the old man seemed to know everything about him; who he was, where he came from, the four suicides. He inquired. "Honey, are you certain everything is alright at home, no problems or anything?"

"Everything is fine Charlie." She replied, "Why wouldn't it be? There is nothing new happening around here since you left, other than the fact I now have to make a special trip into town tomorrow morning and mail your stupid cell phone." She hesitated for a moment he asked again, "Charlie, are you sure you are OK? You sound a little worried?"

"Yes, I am fine. I just hate being half way across the country while you are at home. You know what I mean. Sometimes I get irrationally concerned about you being home alone."

She replied, "There's absolutely nothing to worry about Charlie. You have been traveling all over creation on business for over twenty years and I have never had any problems while you were gone. Why should this trip be any different?"

Charles thought to himself 'different' hardly began to describe the events of this overwhelming business trip. If he truly had experienced all he believed he had in the past few hours, then he had shot an old man through the skull, thinking him a demon, and watched another man devoured by strange creatures conjured up by some sort of sinister cell phone. Yes, 'different' scarcely covered it.

"You're right", Wilson replied trying to sound confident, "I guess I am just a bit exhausted. I am going to try to get a good night's sleep so I can be ready to hit the ground running tomorrow morning. If I seal this deal it will be one of the biggest deals of my career. And it will mean a large commission check for us, as well as a potential promotion for me."

"That would be so great for you, and something you deserve. Good luck with your meeting tomorrow, Honey." She said, "I know how important it is for your career. Be sure to get a good night sleep. I have complete faith in you Charlie and I am sure you will leave the meeting with a signed contract. By the way, your boss, Mr. Edmondson called. He had been trying to reach you. I explained to him you forgot your phone and I would be heading into Yuengsville tomorrow morning and sending it to you overnight. He sounded sort of angry. Maybe you should give him a call first thing tomorrow morning."

"The old fart always sounds angry. He is an irritating pain in the butt, the way he always insists on micromanaging me and checking up on me all of the time. Don't pay any attention to him. He has always been annoying, but since his heart attack last year he has for some reason gotten really bothersome."

Sarah said, "Yes, I remember last year when he was out for about a month after his attack and you filled in for him. You seemed to be in much better spirits, back then as well."

"That was the best month of my career at Edmondson Systems. While he was gone, the place functioned perfectly. I managed to keep everything running smoothly and with less frustration and much less personal stress." Wilson interjected.

"Maybe some day you will have the chance to run the place again. Who knows? Mr. Edmondson isn't getting any younger or any healthier." Sarah suggested.

Charles said, "It would be a nice change, but I seriously doubt the old turd would ever voluntarily give up command of his company. I suspect the only way he will ever leave his office is feet first at room temperature." He gave a gruff laugh then said, "Again, don't concern yourself with his call. It's nothing. The foolish old man can wait for me to call him until after my meeting. Then when I have a signed deal in my hands he will be too busy counting his dollars to bother giving me one of his ridiculous lectures."

His wife chuckled on the other end of the phone then reminded him, "Make sure you call me as soon as you can when the meeting is over. I can't wait to hear the good news."

"I promise I will call you first thing." Wilson said, "Now you be sure to take care honey. I love you."

Charles and his wife said their goodbyes then he hung up the phone. He truly did intend to call his wife after the meeting the next day. However, at the time, neither he nor his wife realized the call would never occur; he would be much too preoccupied to remember to call her. Nor did they know calling her would be an exercise in futility, since by late the next morning, she would be lying dead in a battered heap along a lonely highway.

## Chapter 7

Wilson hung up the phone and sat on the edge of the bed going over every detail of the night's events, as much as his exhausted and half-inebriated mind would allow.

He hoped to figure out exactly what had actually happened this evening, what portion of it was real and what might be imagined, why it happened and specifically why it happened to him. He believed every problem in the world could be solved easily if only people would first look closely at the big problem then break it down into smaller more manageable parts to find the solution. He felt if he broke the night's events down into individual elements, stepped through each one, sorted out what was real and what he might have imagined, he believed he could figure out what to do next to resolve his bizarre situation.

Wilson started with his arrival at the hotel but there appeared to be nothing too eventful or out of the ordinary as he could remember. He had checked into the hotel, then carried his luggage up to his room and put his clothing put away in an organized fashion. He could recall no strange activities during the check-in process, nothing eventful during the elevator ride up to his room, and nothing strange about his room in particular. As far as he could determine, the initial introduction to the hotel was not a problem. The girl at the front desk had been an attractive young thing and did not appear threatening in any way. He continued with his analysis.

Once settled in his room he had decided he had better go out and attempt to find a pre-paid cell phone right away; especially since he was having such rotten luck locating one so far. He had gone back down to the front desk. Yes, that was where things started to get a bit different. The young girl who checked him in was no longer watching the desk. A young man was in her place; one he thought of as a reject from Mickey D's, but he certainly hadn't seem threatening either. Wilson remembered asking the kid where he could buy a cell phone and the young man told him where he might possibly find one... no wait a minute... that was not quite correct either. At last, Wilson felt he might be making some progress.

The young man did not know where to get a phone, but now thinking about it, Wilson recalled there had been a man sitting alone in the lobby reading a newspaper who had walked up to return the paper to the counter mentioning he had overheard Wilson's request. He told Wilson he could buy a phone at any one of several stores down the side street. That was right, Wilson recalled. The stranger was the one who directed him down the dark street, not the clerk at the front desk.

He tried to call to mind what the stranger looked like, but could not. The man must not have had any distinguishing features or else Wilson would surely have noticed such details. However, the more he thought about the man the more he remembered. Wilson believed the man had been over six feet tall and muscular, with dark hair. Then a realization struck him... the robber! The man in the lobby could very well have been the same man in the alley who had tried to assault him.

During the attempted mugging, the robber had told Wilson he was "not an uneducated thug", but he was someone skilled who took pride in his work, who specifically picked and targeted his victims. The man would have known the alley was abandoned and every store was closed. What better way could there have been to lure Wilson into the alley alone? The thief likely waited a few minutes after Wilson left the hotel then followed him down into the side street. He was probably surprised to see Wilson was not in the alley, when he was in fact, inside of the strange store at the time. Wilson assumed the store looked as abandoned to the robber from the outside as it did to Wilson after he had fled the store. So the man must have walked right past the building then turned around and started back toward the hotel in time to see Wilson leave the store and stagger off of the pavement into the street.

Wilson thought for a moment perhaps he might simply be getting paranoid, though not without good reason. Maybe the stranger in the hotel lobby actually was just being a Good Samaritan; pointing Wilson toward what he believed was a solution to his problem. Wilson was not certain the man who had given him the directions was even the same man who had tried to rob him but the logical part of him, not prone to believe in coincidence, thought it might be so. It made no less sense and anything else occurring on this strange evening.

Then Wilson remembered how the inexplicable old store owner had known his name. If the so-called innocent stranger had overheard Wilson checking in, he would have known his name and would have known he was from Pennsylvania. Perhaps the Good Samaritan was not so good after all. Maybe he and the store owner were working together. However, to make such an assumption, Wilson would have to admit to himself the store owner was real and so were the unearthly events which followed. Besides, how could the store owner know about the four men from Wilson's past who had committed suicide? That was something only Wilson knew and kept to himself. Even his wife, Sarah, was unaware of his connection to the four men.

Furthermore, if the robber was working with the store owner, then why had he not known to look for Wilson in the abandoned store? The harder Wilson tried to make sense of everything the less sense everything made. Perhaps he was just too tired, maybe he was losing his mind after all, or possibly, it was the effect of too much whiskey.

Wilson recounted walking down the side street as a light rain had started to fall. By the time he had gotten to the front of the store, the rain had become torrential. He remembered he had not passed a single open store along the way and had looked further down the street, not seeing any sign of activity anywhere else along the dark alley.

He had turned and looked into the store window where he saw the sign advertising prepaid cellular phones. Up until then, nothing had felt odd or out of place, but he remembered as soon as he had entered the store he had begun to get a strange sensation down deep in the pit of his stomach. The hair on the back of his neck had started to stand on end for some unknown reason; it was the type of feeling he got just before a business deal was about to go bad; and that particular deal had certainly gone about as bad as possible.

Wilson tried to remember as many details as he could about the store's interior reviewing them in his mind. Hindsight being twenty-twenty, everything about the store and the old man was wrong from the very beginning and his own intuition had told

him to turn and run long before everything had
gone down the crapper. From then on, his life had
become a surrealistic nightmarish landscape with
penis      grabbing      satanic      statues,      merchants
transforming into demons and muggers sucked into
the bowels of Hell. Bowels of Hell? He stopped for a
second to regroup his thoughts.

## Chapter 8

"Bowels of Hell." He thought once again. Maybe that was it. It felt right, or very wrong depending upon one's perspective. What exactly was the phone? Was it some sort of evil device capable of opening up a portal to another dimension, to another world, or perhaps opening a gateway to Hell itself?

He began to think perhaps his chance arrival at the mysterious antiquities store was not so much by chance but was actually set up in advance, so a series of events could take place for whatever the unknown purpose. That might actually be it. Perhaps he was an unknowing innocent pawn someone or something was using to make a series of events occur. Wilson thought pawn, perhaps, but maybe not so innocent, as he recalled the four suicides once again.

Why him? Why now? Those four men had committed suicide long ago, the most recent being at least five years ago. Why would someone wait so long for some sort of cosmic retribution?

Could it be simply because he had been foolish enough to forget his phone on this trip? No, he did not think so. Suppose he had not forgotten his phone, what then? Then would the scenario play out differently but with the same result? Would someone at the hotel have directed him to a dismal dusty restaurant for dinner where he would find himself the only patron? In addition, would a decrepit old waiter with filthy hands and a torn tee shirt smelling of death and decay have handed him a strange looking blood red menu with chrome skulls on the cover? Then would the waiter have next handed him a gun, then grown into a gigantic demon? Or would someone else have been chosen instead of Wilson? He did not believe so. He believed he was chosen and no matter what the scenario, he was somehow destined to play a role. He wondered if perhaps there was some sort of tarnished aura surrounding him; only certain people could see which marked him as the one to choose. Perhaps he was damaged goods; a blemished soul.

Moreover, why had he forgotten his phone anyway? He never forgot his phone. Why did he do so this time? Could these unknown forces have been at work all the way back in Pennsylvania, before he even left for this trip? Had these forces caused him to forget his phone on purpose, in order to assure he would end up in that particular store and in that particular alley? The idea of some mysterious power could have so much control over his life was too much for Wilson to comprehend.

And what about the dreadful looking damned phone? "Damned indeed," he heard the old storekeeper say in his mind. Wilson shuddered. What was he supposed to do with the phone anyway? He had seen some of what it was capable of this evening and it horrified him. But, what did it have to do with him specifically? He had no use for such a device. He was an executive, a family man, not some common street thug. What would he do with such power? Then he thought about it again, power. Yes, the phone did have incredible power, which meant the holder of the phone also possessed and controlled the power.

He recalled how when the robber had threatened him, all he had managed to do was press one of those single skull shaped buttons then all Hell broke loose, literally. He had no idea if he had actually pressed the '9' button as he had intended or which button he had pressed. He suspected no matter which button he would have pressed the results would have been the same.

He supposed it might have happened even if he hadn't actually pressed a button but simply held the phone in his hand. Wilson recalled how just before pressing the button, a rage of anger greater than he believed he could ever muster welled up inside of him. He somehow instinctively understood the buttons, like the phone itself were just symbolic, not actually functional. The real power of the phone came from somewhere much deeper inside. "Deeper inside?" He thought about it for a few moments. Then he wondered, deeper inside of the phone... or deeper inside himself?

Wilson recalled the scene, as the flayed dying body of the robber was being drug into the opening in the world while the man screamed in his final agony. Then Wilson remembered hearing the old man's voice saying the phrase that Wilson recalled from Sunday school, "Well done, my good and faithful servant." Why would such an evil creature use such a well known biblical phrase? However, wasn't the phrase just that, a series of words put together to express a thought? The phrase did not have to be reserved only for biblical usage; anyone could use the expression as he chose. However, hearing the well-known phrase used in the context of the awful phone, and in the voice of the disgusting old man, made Wilson feel sick.

And why 'servant'? Wilson did not like the idea of thinking of himself as anyone's servant, especially a servant to some sort of demonic force from Hell, or some creature from another dimension.

It was then he recounted the old man asking Wilson to kill him so he could go be with his master. Was the old man's purpose simply to pass the phone on to Wilson? Was the phone the property of this mysterious master? Was that why the old man had only one cell phone available? Was the old man the previous keeper of the phone? Or more disturbingly, had he been a servant to the phone?

When Wilson had inquired about the pre-loaded minutes and features the phone may have had, the old man said simply, "It has whatever you will need." Whatever he would need? What was that supposed to mean? Was Wilson now somehow bound to the same master as the old storekeeper may have been? If so, did using the phone bind him to its unknown purpose?

He contemplated if had he not used the phone, perhaps he would have been spared any such connection. He may not have used the phone with initial hostile intent but he had used it to try to summon help in an unfortunate situation. In addition, did he actually use the phone or did the phone use him? Did the phone reach down inside of Wilson somehow and control him, causing his anger to rise to an almost uncontrollable degree. Did it actually force his finger to press the button?

Wilson pondered how significantly his life had changed over the past few hours. He had been personally responsible for the deaths of two individuals, the old storekeeper and the mugger; if not directly or intentionally, then at least indirectly and unintentionally. Then once again, he thought of the old man accusing him of causing four suicides. It appeared to Wilson the bodies were piling up. Charlie Wilson, who had thought of himself as a gentle man, who never hunted, fished or hurt a living creature, was now a killer. Or was he?

And what about the robber? Wilson had not wished him any harm to him. He was simply trying to dial 911 when the very fabric of reality opened up and sucked the man inside of the flaming black slit, while all those horrid little worm-things feasted on the charred remains of the thug's flesh.

Looking intently across the room at the phone on the desk, Wilson summarized the only thing he actually did know for certain, was he somehow had acquired a pre-paid cell phone, and an ugly pre-paid cell phone at that. Everything else may or may not have actually happened. For all he knew he may have simply found the cell phone on his way into the alley, looked into the darkness of the street, thought better of going down there and simply turned around to return to the hotel. Everything else may have been his imagination; some sort of blackout, seizure or hallucination. He certainly did have a very active imagination. Maybe he was developing a brain tumor. He would have to remember to make an appointment with his doctor when he returned home and have his brain scanned.

The analytical part of Charles Wilson needed to find a way to rationalize the events of the evening into something concrete he could quantify and understand. All the while, his gut, his primal flight or flight instinct was screaming for him to understand the severity of the situation. His analytical side won the day rationalizing the things he thought he saw this evening he simply could not have seen.

Maybe he could not understand everything but he did understand he was a lucid, sane man who worked in a world of facts, figures, balance sheets and bottom lines; and the bottom line here was demons and rips in reality simply were not possible. Yes, he decided a trip to his doctor was definitely in order when he returned home. Wilson poured himself another glass of whiskey feeling confident now none of this could possibly have been real. He breathed a long sigh of relief.

Then the cell phone began to ring.

# Chapter 9

Wilson sat stock still, not sure what to do next. The accursed cell phone was ringing and vibrating on the dresser across the room. He wondered if he should answer it, or perhaps he should ignore it. If he had actually found the phone somewhere then the call might be coming from a friend or relative of the owner, or perhaps the owner himself calling from another phone. If, however, the 'other' events of the evening, the horrible and unspeakable events surrounding this phone had actually occurred, then the last thing Wilson wanted to do was answer the phone.

The phone continued to ring...

He wondered if he touched the flesh-like skin of the phone would the fabric of reality open up once again like a flaming wound and pull him inside this time, screaming, as his own flesh was burned from his body.

The phone continued to ring...

Wilson took another long drink of whiskey then slowly, cautiously, slid off the bed and walked hesitantly toward the phone, still uncertain if he would actually answer it or not. He approached the dresser and stood staring down at the phone's blood red cover, those hideous grinning chrome skull keys and the red glow coming from the screen where the message 'Unknown Caller' appeared. Wilson reached his hand out slowly, as if getting ready to answer the phone then thought better of it and pulled his hand back as if recoiling from a potential bite from a venomous snake.

The phone continued to ring...

Wilson made up his mind he would not answer the phone. In fact, he would never answer the phone. It could ring from now until doomsday but he would not answer it. He turned to head back to the bed when suddenly a searing pain struck inside of his skull the likes of which he had never experienced in his life. His ears rang with a high-pitched whine adding increased agony to the already unbearable suffering. Wilson had experienced a few severe migraines in his day, but even the worst could not compare with the pain he felt now.

He fell to his knees as the strength left his legs, grabbing helplessly at the sides of his head as if somehow, through this empty gesture, he would be able to cause the pain to go away. Or, perhaps he was unconsciously trying to keep his brains from oozing from his skull through his ears and dribbling onto the floor in a gelatinous puddle.

In his pain-riddled mind, he heard a voice, which sounded like the voice of that old man from the store. The voice was a faint raspy caw, which at first was indecipherable, and then Wilson realized the voice was ordering him to go back and pick up the phone. The voice said "answer the phone ... answer it ... answer it ....Wilson...or you will... suffer this... excruciating pain .. until ...your brain... turns to puss." The voice sounded as if it was straining to get through to him, as if this particular form of telepathic communication was too difficult for the voice to maintain for very long. But Wilson understood the pain he was feeling was so strong and so intense his brain would turn to mush and he would die in agony shortly if he did not do something to stop the misery.

He felt as though his head would explode from the pain as he staggered to his feet stumbling back toward the phone, vibrating and ringing angrily on the dresser. The last thing he wanted to do was reach out for that accursed phone but the agony in his skull was so unbearable he was sure by now, blood must be pouring from his ears, though when he pulled his hands away they were free of any crimson fluid.

He reluctantly reached out his hand and as soon as the tips of his fingers touched the cover of the phone the ringing stopped and the pain in his head vanished just as instantaneously as it had arrived. It was completely gone with no trace of having ever been there, no dull throbbing he normally felt after a migraine; nothing. He picked up the phone looking for an answer button but could not find one. Instead, he heard the distant voice of the old storekeeper again, this time coming through the phone saying, "Very good Mr. Wilson. Your touch was all you needed to answer the phone. Now pay heed to what I tell you for my time is short."

With that, Wilson lifted the phone and slowly placed it hesitantly to his ear. For a moment he imagined as the phone got close to his ear, hundreds of fleshy filaments would burst through from the speaker, encasing his skull and face, penetrating his ear and boring deep into his brain. Once there the strands would lay eggs so their vile offspring could slowly feast on his grey matter, as he lay in a vegetative state on the floor of his hotel in a pool of his own blood, urine and drool.

However, this was not the case. When Wilson did place the phone to his ear, he experienced something almost as appalling. He felt revulsion at the feel of the flesh like phone against his cheek. It was as if a thousand maggots were crawling along the surface of his face. The phone has an internal pulse made Wilson feel as if it were alive, and perhaps it was. He pulled the phone away from his face slightly and held back the sudden urge to vomit. Instead, he placed it closer to his ear, being careful not to touch his skin, and listened to hear what message he was meant to receive.

"Good evening once again Mr. Wilson," said the voice from inside the phone, which was definitely the old storekeeper's. Wilson said nothing and simply waited for the voice to continue. He did not wish to entertain any conversation with this demonic being. His nostrils still seemed to hold the rancid reek of the old man's foul and horrid scent.

The voice said. "And thank you so very much for completing the task for which you were chosen; for freeing me from my earthly shackles, allowing me to fulfill my own personal destiny."

Wilson cared nothing for this man's personal destiny or for anything else the horrid creature had to say. The old man had already caused him more anguish in the past hours than he cared to think about. When Wilson could hold out no longer he shouted into the phone "What the Hell is this all about? Who are you? What is this phone? Why are you doing this to me?"

The voice interrupted "All in good time Mr. Wilson; all in good time. For now, all you need to know is you have been chosen."

Again Wilson was frustrated by the cryptic way in which the old man spoke. "Chosen? Chosen for what? Who are you?" Wilson asked again. "Are you really the old man from the store? That foul and disgusting creature I killed. Didn't you die? I am sure I saw you die. What's is going on?"

Again the voice replied "As I said Mr. Wilson, all in good time. For now, all you need to know is you have been designated to be the keeper of the phone. This is a great honor and a great responsibility."

"Keeper of the phone? But I don't want the responsibility. And I don't consider this any honor." Wilson protested. "I don't want any more to do with any of this!"

# Chapter 10

"What we want is not always what we get, Mr. Wilson," the aged voice continued. "Our actions, however, often do dictate what we end up getting. How many times in your business dealings did you manage to get exactly what you wanted while your clients, customers and business partners got, shall we say, the short end of the stick."

"Why...almost all of the time." Wilson said arrogantly. "I pride myself on never making a bad deal. I always come out on top in any business proposition. It is what makes me so good at what I do and so successful."

The old man continued. "Exactly. You never make a bad deal. You always win. You always come out on top, no matter what happens to the other party and no matter whom you might hurt in the process. Remember O'Connell, Gladstone, Dawson and Johnson?" Once again, the old man brought up the four suicides. "You essentially killed them even though you didn't do the actual deed. Your actions are the reason they are dead."

"They were weak." Wilson insisted, "They killed themselves. I did nothing. You don't understand. You are just a foolish old man. It is a dog-eat-dog world out there; survival of the fittest. Kill or be killed. The business world may not be pretty at times but survival at all costs is what it is all about."

"On the contrary, Mr. Wilson, I understand completely." The old man interrupted, "Oh yes, I understand better than you may realize. I am not criticizing you for your actions. It is that attitude which has brought us together in the first place. It is what has led you to us and to the honor, which we have bestowed upon you. You are the keeper of the phone."

"The damned phone again! What about this phone? Tell me more." Wilson inquired. "What is its purpose?"

The voice on the phone hesitated for an instant then replied, "It is a most sacred and precious relic. It is ageless. It will be whatever it is needed to be to accomplish the goal the must be completed. Its form and purpose is always defined by the user."

"What does that mean?" Wilson demanded.

"Soon all will become clear." The old man responded.

Then the phone went dead. Wilson stood staring at the now silent phone. He repeated aloud "The purpose of the phone is defined by the user." He wondered what that was supposed to mean. It made no sense to him at all. If the user defined the purpose of the phone and he was to be the user then why, when he wanted the phone to dial 911 had the phone reacted so savagely? He did not ask the world to open up a gaping wound and for evil crawling creatures to pull his assailant into oblivion, yet that is what had happened. All he had wanted to do was to call for help.

Or was it really true? On the surface, perhaps, but deep down inside, down in the primitive reptilian portion of his brain hadn't he wanted to see the man suffer? In his gut, he had hated the man for threatening him, humiliating him, essentially violating his manhood by making him feel helpless and trying to steal his personal belongings. Deep down inside he had a boiling cauldron of hatred perhaps the phone could see and use.

Maybe he had even subconsciously thought the words "Go to Hell." Had he thought those words? Wilson did not believe so, but he was uncertain. Could this hatred have been so strong, although he could not see, somehow the phone could? If he simply thought the words, "Go to Hell" would a gateway to Hell would open up and swallow anyone he chose? He did not think so. He thought it might be a bit more complicated.

Wilson wondered for a moment if he could command the phone to open up a gateway to Heaven or perhaps a portal to Omaha or Hawaii or wherever. Somehow, he did not believe that was the case either. He thought this phone opened up one portal and only one, and the portal was to a place of incredible suffering and torture. There was only one destination using this phone... Hell itself.

Initially, he believed the horrid phone was incapable of doing any good for society whatsoever. It was only capable of evil. Now that he had some time to reflect; to think a bit more, he began to change his mind ever so slightly.

When he used the phone to inadvertently eliminate the mugger, hadn't the phone indirectly done some societal good? Hadn't it rid the earth of a robber, a villain, someone who preyed on the good people of society? Granted, the way in which the phone had dispatched the thug was pure evil, but hadn't he served the greater good of society ultimately, by the elimination of this treacherous being from the earth? Yes he believed maybe it had done just that.

He thought of his college economics class and about the principle of the 'unseen hand' which miraculously turned acts of individual selfishness into acts that would eventually benefit society in the end.

He began to imagine with proper handling and control, the phone could be used to rid the world of some of its most vile criminals. But at what cost he wondered? If he knowingly used the phone to murder the criminals of the world wouldn't he then become one of the very criminals he chose to eliminate? Then would the phone in turn eliminate him? This was another paradox for him to consider.

With this latest revelation he comprehended the only solutions the phone could offer, were final solutions; death. He recalled the old man's words in the store earlier in the evening "The price for the phone is one death."

Wilson contemplated if that statement meant the price to take possession of the phone was one death or the price to use the phone was one death, and was it one death each time someone used the phone? Could the phone take more than one person? He did not know. Did it only take the guilty or did it take innocents along with it? He did not believe the phone or the force behind it cared one way or the other. Could he use it to wipe out an entire army or an entire country? He did not think so unless perhaps the hatred the he felt was great enough. He believed the phone needed to have a personal connection. The user needed to personally feel ultimate hatred deep down inside to make the phone do his bidding. On the other hand, was it as if the phone was sensing the user's hatred and making the user do its bidding? Wilson's mind spun with questions.

The old man on the phone had said it was a sacred relic and it was ageless. He had hinted although the relic now took the form of a cell phone now it could very well have taken an entirely different form a thousand years ago. "It is ageless. It is whatever it needs to be." Wilson said aloud summarizing what the old man had said.

He also suspected if he pressed one of the skull buttons right now, with no purpose in mind, nothing would happen at all. Wilson reached out and took another swig from his glass of whiskey.

Wilson held the phone in his hand and reached his thumb around cautiously to press a button. He hesitated for just a second then pressed the 'six' key. He closed his eyes and gritted his teeth waiting to see if something happened but it did not. He laughed to himself. Maybe he actually was losing his mind; maybe he was drunker than he thought. He hoped against all hope all of this was just a bad dream from which he might awaken at any moment.

He set the phone on the bedspread, sat down next to it and grabbed the remote control to turn on the hotel television. Maybe all he needed was a few moments of mind-numbing television combined with his mind-numbing drink, to help him relax and perhaps salvage enough of this evening so he might be able to get a good night's sleep after all.

The television came on displaying the cable guide, which Wilson ignored, pressing the channel change button to surf for anything of interest. After a few clicks, he saw a news bulletin appear on the screen. It flashed the words "LIVE LATE BREAKING NATIONAL NEWS" across the bottom of the screen while above the words he saw a man in an orange jump suit being led handcuffed and shackled through a crowd of reporters apparently on the way to a police car in the nearby parking lot.

The camera panned to the front facade of a courthouse with many tall thin windows, stone face and rounded arch glass entryway. Wilson thought he recognized the courthouse. Another even more distant view flashed on the television with a shot of the four-sided clock tower looming high above the street below. Wilson was sure he had seen the courthouse before. Then the camera returned to the view of the reporters and police at the top of the courthouse stairs.

A broadcast news reporter's voice over came on saying; "This is Bill Pierson coming to you live from the Schuylkill County Courthouse in Yuengsville, PA." Wilson suddenly understood why he recognized the building; it was the courthouse in his hometown. The reporter continued, "Where at this very moment, following a special late night court session, Randal Lee Forester is being led away by police, after being sentenced to life in prison based on his conviction for the August 19th, 2007 rape and murder of two-year-old Jennifer Lynn Stanton, the daughter of his then live-in girlfriend, Marie Louise Stanton. It is believed the sentencing was scheduled for this late hour, in an attempt to reduce the media coverage of the event, but as you can see by the number of news outlets present, this attempt was not very effective. Forester's attorneys stated the appeal process has already begun and feel confident the conviction and sentence will be overturned within the next year."

Wilson's face reddened with rage as he screamed at the set, "That son of a bitch should fry for what he did." He watched the guards guide the man through the crowds across to the courthouse parking lot.

He recalled how the story had originally broken locally in Schuylkill County but, due to the horrendous nature of the crime, it had gotten worldwide coverage. Wilson was disgusted by the amount of media coverage involved. In his opinion, the vultures of the news media loved this kind of despicable story and although he understood it was their job and responsibility to report such events, and he still hated them for it.

Wilson remembered the events leading up to the baby's murder. How the news stories reported Forester had been sexually, and physically abusing the baby since birth, and how her mother had done nothing to stop him. The mother had claimed to police she was too afraid of Forester to try to stop him, but later it was discovered she was a heavy drug user and was, for the most part, oblivious to what Forester was doing.

To date, no charges had been filed against the girl friend but reporters suspected charges of child negligence would be filed soon. "That bastard should suffer long and hard for what he did to that poor little girl." Wilson shouted drunkenly at the television screen, his anger and rage increasing.

Wilson heard a buzzing sound next to him and noticed the light on the cell phone's screen glowing with bright red illumination. Wilson looked at the screen where the message 'NOW' appeared. He looked back at the television; his fury now exploding into a drunken rage, and without forethought picked up the phone, pointed it directly at the television and randomly pressed a skull key, his anger once again seeming to flow into the phone.

On television, the live feed picture began to shake and blur as the ground around the precession of police officers and reporters began to quake. The news reporter announced in an alarming voice, "There seems to be some sort of disturbance occurring. The ground is shaking like crazy. I suspect we are experiencing an earthquake." The camera continued filming the procession with its now jerky motion.

About ten feet in front of the procession, which had reached the courthouse parking lot, the ground began to crack open as an enormous fracture formed in the asphalt. The officers guarding Forester dove to the right and left to avoid being pulled down into the widening crevasse while everyone around and behind him did likewise.

The rapist/murderer Forester stood motionless as if he were incapable of making any attempt to save himself as the ever-lengthening fissure made its way toward him, now reaching over thirty feet long. Smoke and flames began to shoot high upward out of the opening. The sides of the massive slit glowed bright red where they met the black top, as the asphalt bubbled and dripped molten black tar down into the hole.

When the opening reached the place where Forester stood, the man began to sink downward, stiff as a board, into the opening. Reptilian tentacles with claw like hands reached upward from the opening covering Forester's lower legs setting his orange jump suit afire. The man screamed in pain as the flesh beneath the suit liquefied and slid from his legs. The flames from the jumpsuit spread upward engulfing his upper body and setting his hair ablaze. Below, from deep in the crevasse, hundreds of spider like creatures skittered from the opening climbing up the burning man's body, moving right though the flames completely unaffected by their searing heat.

The camera zoomed in close to the screaming man's face as several of the spider creatures slid inside his wide-open mouth. Wilson saw one of Forester's eyeballs pop from its socket and dangle down on his cheek as the spider thing crawled out of the bleeding orifice. The spider creature looked directly at the camera. Wilson felt it was looking directly at him and he was horrified beyond all comprehension to see the thing had a face; a tiny hideous human-like face, and the face resembled that of himself, Charles Wilson.

It reminded him of the scene at the end of the original 1958 Sci-Fi movie, "The Fly" where actor, David Hedison's head was shown on the body of the fly trapped in a spider's web as the spider approached to devour him. The helpless human/fly screamed, "Help me. Help me," over and over. Charles had seen the movie on television as a young boy and that particular scene had haunted his nightmares for months. Now this human/Charles headed creature was not crying for help; it was instead devouring the burning flesh and perhaps very soul of the dying Randal Lee Forester.

On the verge of passing out from the horrific spectacle unfolding before him, Wilson somehow managed to maintain consciousness perhaps with the morbid curiosity of someone watching a train wreck; sickened, but unable to look away. He saw a hairy leg protruding from the dying man's nostril grabbing his upper lip and ripping a bloody strip of skin free, pulling it up into the nostril where it shoved it deep into its hungry maw. Forester's hair was ablaze as the spider things crawled into his ears and burrowed deep inside his skull cavity.

The body continued slowly sinking into the abyss as Forester screamed and cried for mercy. As soon as it had slid completely down into the opening, there was another tremendous earthquake and the crack began to fuse back together, sealing Forester inside for eternity. When the ground stopped shaking there was not a single sign remaining to indicate the opening had ever existed. There was not a crack, not a split or not even a bulge in the asphalt. It was as smooth as if it had just been poured by a crew of professionals.

Wilson sat in shock, revolted by what he had just witnessed, by what he believed he had just made happen. But, had he actually done it? He was a thousand miles from Pennsylvania yet somehow his hatred of the despicable piece of human refuse, Forester, was so great the phone had done its work, done his work, even at such a great distance. And not only had he witnessed the event, but half of America if not the world, witnessed it as well.

Before he could even begin to understand what had just happened, the TV station, which had gone on an emergency commercial break, returned with replay footage of the event.

Once again, unable to look away, Wilson watched the repeat of the incident on the news program, certain this event would likely replay on every major worldwide market within the hour and for the next week as well, until something more ghastly and therefore more interesting took its place, somewhere else in the world. However, what Wilson saw on the replay was considerably different from what he had actually witnessed when watching the event live.

On the replay footage, the earthquake occurred as originally seen and the crack in the earth opened up as well, but was where the similarity ended. In the replay, Wilson did not see any flames or melting asphalt. He saw no reptilian arms with clawed human-like hands, no flames or no skittering Charles-faced spider creatures. What he saw was simply Forester sliding down into the crack screaming for help as he sunk below the surface, and the quake closed the opening sealing him inside. Although the site of the man's death on film was still extremely graphic, perhaps too graphic for prime time television, and the man's cries were haunting, the horror depicted was not a fraction of what Wilson had witnessed.

Wilson was dumbfounded. He knew what he had seen, he was certain of what he had witnessed, yet when he watched the replay video none of the creatures were there. How could this be? Wilson's mind again began to swim but this time much worse than before, his vision became blurred, the room began to spin and he passed out, falling backward onto the hotel bed cover.

In the days to follow, the county workers would be given the task of jack hammering through a large portion of the asphalt on the courthouse parking lot in a feeble attempt to try to recover Forester's body but it would never be found. There would never be a good scientific explanation for what had happened, and how could there be?

Forester was in a very special place in Hell where he would be suffering for millions of years after all of the people who morbidly watched his disappearance had died and turned to dust.

Newspapers over the next few days would flash headlines such as "Divine Justice", "Heavenly Retribution" and "Justice Served By God" as the television broadcasts played and replayed the footage. Church attendance would increase for several months to come. The town of Yuengsville would have to add auxiliary police to watch the courthouse parking lot round the clock for several months, as thousands of people from around the world made pilgrimages to see the site where the alleged divine retribution had taken place. Scientists would offer their logical theories as to what had happened, but it would not stop the superstitions.

Eventually the incident would reach folk legend status and the video clips would end up on various mystery specials and "Ripley's Believe It Or Not" types of television shows. Most rational thinking people would consider it one of those strange natural occurrences or coincidences and eventually would simply forget about it. And no matter how many times the video was seen and no matter how closely it was scrutinized, no one anywhere would ever see what Charles Wilson had seen that night, for only he could see the truth, because he was the keeper of the phone.

# Chapter II

After collapsing into an unconscious heap on the hotel bed, Charles Wilson did not have a pleasant night's sleep as he had hoped, but instead found his slumber tormented with scenes of horror spanning countless centuries. These images accosted him throughout the night in a rapid-fire series of terrible nightmares from which he was unable to awaken as he was forced to watch violent events, one more gruesome than the next, play out upon his dream scape.

Flash...Wilson found he could not speak. In his mind, he heard the words he wished to utter aloud but when he tried to articulate them all he was able to generate were a few guttural sounding grunts. It was as if he did not have vocal chords sufficient to utter speech. He did not understand why he was no longer capable of doing something as simple as saying a few words. He noticed in addition, he was sitting in a place of almost complete darkness with only traces of glowing light coming from the ground directly in front of him.

As things slowly began to come into focus, Wilson looked around the murky environment and saw he was outdoors and it was an exceptionally dark night. The minimal glowing light available came from what appeared to be hot embers remaining in was once must have been a campfire enclosed in a circle of rocks. He could smell the acrid aroma of burning wood and saw the charcoals glowing brightly in the fire pit. He seemed to be alone at the campfire, not seeing any other shadows encircling the area.

He looked up toward the heavens and saw a quarter-moon high in the night sky along with thousands of brightly shining stars sparkling like precious jewels against a coal black background. He had never seen a more spectacular sight in his life; realizing the reason the view was so incredible was there was literally no illumination from any surrounding towns. Such light pollution generally prevented urban dwellers from seeing such a beautiful sight. The stars were so amazingly stunning Wilson felt he easily could have spent the rest of his life sitting and staring at them, perhaps counting them one by one or creating his own constellation patterns by playing connect the stars. The entire awe-inspiring experience left Wilson breathless.

Then he felt a icy breeze blow across his body making him feel naked and defenseless against the elements. As his eyes began to adjust to the darkness, Wilson noticed some loose logs lying within reach. He picked up a large piece of dried branch, which had a number of dried leaves attached and placed it atop the red-hot coals. He also found some dried grass on a pile next to him, which once added to the embers, quickly burst into flames igniting the dried log bringing the fire roaring back to life. He added a few additional logs from the pile and within a few moments, the roaring fire provided the much-needed warmth. Wilson was somewhat surprised by his own strength and how he had easily tossed the logs onto the fire without ever getting up from his sitting position.

The now blazing fire provided some light for Wilson to get a better feel for his surroundings. He could now see his arms the firelight and was stunned to notice they did not seem to be his arms at all, but were instead, much larger, more muscular and covered with long thick black almost animal-like hair. He found this revelation to be very disconcerting. These huge arms also seemed to be grimy with some sort of dried mud or caked-on dirt, as if he had gone a long time without bathing.

His also noticed his field of vision was somewhat impaired by what appeared to be extremely long strands of filthy, greasy black hair dangling in disarray from his forehead. He raised what he discovered to be one of his massive hands and roughly finger-combed the hair back out of his eyes slicking the slimy mass backward, hearing it slap against the top of his huge head. He also seemed to have itching sensation not only on his scalp, but all over his body. He noticed a foul animal-like feral woodsy odor and was embarrassed to realize the scent was actually coming from him.

He became aware he was sitting squat on a large hard rock in front of the now roaring fire, covered in what appeared to be the skin of some type of wild animal. Thinking about what he had observed so far, he appeared to be not much more than an animal, himself, draped in hides, itching and smelling of filth. He realized he was not the same Charles Wilson he once was, but actually seemed to be occupying the body of some sort of primitive being, perhaps what he thought of as a cave man. He wondered how and why he was inside the body of a primitive creature such as this.

Wilson looked down between his massive hair-covered legs and saw huge almost furry bare feet with gnarled, thick, yellowed and blackened toenails. Sitting on the ground between the large feet, he noticed what appeared at first glance to be a human skull. Upon closer examination, Wilson realized it was too small to be an actual skull but was in fact, a primitive carving of a skull apparently made from a large chunk of stone or quartz crystal.

He reached down and picked up the skull, holding it in the palm of his huge hand. In the place where the empty eye sockets should have been, two ruby-red jewels were pressed into the stone. He turned the skull over in his hand as was surprised to see the jewels did not fall from the sockets. Wilson looked and them closer, marveling at the time and craftsmanship that must have gone into hand grinding the sockets and mating jewels to get such a tight and precise fit. He never would have imagined such a precise sculpture could have been created in what was apparently a primitive environment. He instinctively knew he, or the creature who's body he now occupied, did not create this magnificent work of art, but somehow he was nonetheless in possession and apparently in control of it. He placed the skull back on the ground between his feet.

Wilson heard what sounded like the grunting of a group of animals, perhaps wild pigs, coming out the darkness beyond the reach of the firelight. Suddenly, three huge hairy humanoid creatures, rippling with muscles; filthy with mud and covered with grime lurched quickly toward his fire, their sweat-covered frames glistening in the firelight. Their darting, cautious movements reminded Wilson of the actions he had seen gorillas make during his visit the previous year to the Philadelphia Zoo. Yet these beasts were not quite gorillas or apes but some prehistoric form of early man. They seemed to dart toward his fire howling, screaming and waving their arms, and then just as quickly, they would retreat backward into the darkness, only to dart back out once again. It appeared as if they were both amazed and yet somehow terrified by the sight of the blazing fire.

They continued this strange forward and backward process for several minutes, daring to get a little bit closer to the fire with each subsequent approach as Wilson sat quietly, continuing to study their actions with utter fascination. He had a sense these three beings were perhaps a different version of the type of being he appeared to be, perhaps more primitive and obviously less intelligent category, but they were beyond a doubt much larger and quite possibly much stronger.

They shouted a series of howls, cries and grunts at Wilson as if they were unhappy with him and were taunting him for some unknown reason. Perhaps they were jealous of the fact he had fire and they did not. Perhaps they wanted possession of the fire or perhaps they simply feared the fire. Maybe their actions were based on some long-standing feud between rival clans. Wilson did not know and could not determine this from their rapid movements in and out of the shadows.

He was able to conclude one of the creatures in particular must have been the leader of the group. The being was an enormous beast, larger than the other two, with long incredibly muscular arms practically dragging on the ground. From what Wilson could determine, he too was clothed in the skin of some sort of animal. Wilson could not see the details of his face but could see the creature's hair was long and matted and his face was covered with a fur-like beard under a large bulbous nose, protruding forehead and thick furry brow. The being waived his large arms high in the air. His suspicions of this horrid creature's leadership were confirmed further in the way the other beasts seem to stay back in the shadows until his actions seemed to signal it was safe to venture out.

Wilson noticed glimpses of something strange as the creatures darted in and out of the firelight; something suspended from the massive hand of the leader of the beasts. When the creature made one of his charges toward the fire, Wilson could determine in one arm the creature held some type of primitive ax. It appeared to be a long wooden club, which was Y-shaped near the top, with a sharp edged rock fastened into the end of the club. It was held in place by a series of interlaced straps of perhaps animal hide. The sharp edge of the ax appeared to be covered with what looked like clumps of flesh, and was stained crimson, caked with coppery drying blood.

Suddenly all of the brutes started to whoop and howl as one, and the lead creature charged forward once again from the darkness, having put down the ax, now waiving something else high in the air and dangling it apparently for Wilson to see. The savage held what looked like the severed head of another creature such as himself; perhaps a female. Although disgusted by the display, Wilson did not initially comprehend its significance, other than the fact this pack obviously had slaughtered some other creature and was taunting Wilson for some reason with its severed head.

At first, he did not understand why they would be doing such a thing. Then with the sudden recognition of the creature who's body Wilson was occupying, he understood the head the lead beast was swinging about was not some random being but was actually that of this Wilson creature's own mate. These savages had apparently murdered and decapitated her and were waving their prize at Wilson to taunt him into some sort of physical confrontation with it.

Wilson could feel his anger growing, or more appropriately, the anger of the host creature, rising more furiously by the moment, taking the heartache the creature felt at the loss of his mate and transforming it into savage animal rage.

Next Wilson felt a sharp pain against his head and realized one of the taunting creatures hiding back in the darkness must have thrown a rock, striking him on the skull. Blood trickled down his forehead into his right eye. At first Wilson was unsure what to do as he was both confused by the situation and somehow felt overcome with unbearable sorrow over the discovery of this being's murdered mate, as if it were his own wife that had been killed.

Soon the grief was replaced by the fuming anger, so savage Wilson could scarcely comprehend it. There had been many times in his life when he had felt angry enough to perhaps even kill someone, yet even his worst anger could not compare with the pure frenzy he now was feeling. He reached down and grabbed the skull carving on the ground, determined to hurl it at one of the huge beings as soon as one of them came back into the firelight.

The skull began pulsing in his hand and for a moment, Wilson almost dropped it into the fire as it felt as if thousands of creeping insects were moving beneath his grasp. But he was unable to let go. The skull's ruby eyes began to glow in the firelight.

When the savages stumbled out of the darkness next, their backs were toward Wilson and they were facing back into the darkness walking in reverse toward him. He realized they were backing away from something in the darkness so frightening even these ferocious creatures were horrified by its presence. They were all howling and screaming again but these were no longer the frenzied war whoops Wilson had heard earlier; instead these were cries of terror and pain.

In the firelight Wilson saw the leader of the beasts who was screaming the loudest had long smoldering tentacles wrapped around his arms, legs and neck burning through his flesh clean to the bone and seemed to be pulling him back into the darkness. In the distance, Wilson could see through the blackness that a huge opening had erupted in the ground. The edges of the opening were distinguishable in the blackness as they glowed white-hot. A foul stench filled the air along with the screams of the huge male whose flesh was melting from his body. The tentacle surrounding the creature's neck burned its way through to the neck bone and the brute stopped his cries of pain as his head fell to the ground. Wilson heard the skittering of clawed feet as spider like creatures emerged from the darkness to carry away the dead beast's severed head. He could not make out the faces of these spider creatures in the darkness but somehow he suspected they would have human-like faces resembling the cave creature possessing the skull.

With accompanying cries of anguish, the other two members of the pack were likewise pulled backward into the darkness as Wilson watched the crack in the earth begin to fuse back together and the white-hot light disappeared....

## Chapter 12

Flash ...Wilson next found himself standing on an expansive stone patio of some sort, overlooking a sand-covered area of a desert region appearing to go on for miles in every direction. The sun had set, and a full moon illuminated the area below him, where thousands of torches sparkled like stars against the desert sand. He seemed to be looking down on some sort of building site, where what looked like an enormous Egyptian-styled temple was under construction. At the area closest to him, he could see thousands of people below working feverishly under the lash of hundreds of overseers. It was apparent to Wilson these workers were slaves, not only by their pitiful physical conditions, but also by the inhumane treatment they were receiving. These unfortunates seemed to cover the spectrum of ages ranging from very young children to old men and women, some crippled and barely able to walk. Their clothing hung tattered like rags from their emaciated bodies. Wilson could hear the overseers slashing whips and the screams of anguish echoing through the moonlit night.

Wilson realized he was no longer in the body of the primitive beast from a few moments ago, but now seemed to be looking though the eyes of someone of a less ancient time and apparently someone of great importance. He stood alone on the huge patio. This person was someone he understood to be in charge of the activities taking place below. He looked about the expanse of the patio where he stood, astonished at its incredible size and grandeur, made of some highly polished stone, etched and decorated with ornate designs. Around the patio, large pillars perhaps six feet in diameter soared over fifty feet into the air supporting a huge ceiling adorned with paintings depicting incredibly violent acts of murder, sodomy, fornication and debauchery. He found this all quite disturbing. What sort of creature would allow such blasphemous and blatantly filthy works of art to grace the ceiling of their home for the entire world to see?

He examined himself by the moonlight and noticed his arms were no longer huge and hairy but were now slim and virtually free of muscle tone or hair. He looked downward and was shocked to see a lovely set of voluptuous female breasts, draped in some sort of wrap-around dress, hung from his chest and continued downward to a very shapely body. This was extremely disconcerting to say the least. Wilson realized he was looking through the eyes of a female, a young, probably attractive and obviously important female.

Wilson felt something in his right hand and noticed he held a long wooden staff perhaps seven feet tall. At the top of the staff was a shining silver amulet embossed with a skull with ruby red eyes reflecting the moonlight.

Behind him, Wilson heard a noise as someone approached from inside the building, perhaps a palace, to which the outside porch was attached. Without speaking, he turned slowly and faced a large muscular man who stood in a menacing attack pose holding a sword at the ready. Wilson understood through the mind of this female, the man was someone who was the supervisor of the overseers working below. He also knew this man had been a trusted servant of this woman's royal family, but for some reason Wilson sensed things had suddenly changed and the female body he occupied was in grave danger from this person. The man spoke in a tongue Wilson had never heard before, yet somehow he understood every word the angry man uttered as if the man were speaking English.

The man shouted, with anger and apparent sadness "I am so sorry, my Queen. Though I have served you faithfully for my entire life, I can no longer do so. The unspeakable acts you have committed upon your own people are beyond human understanding. I suspect your heart is black and your mind is riddled with maggots. You have come to represent the epitome of pure evil. Your people, your subjects, say perhaps you are a witch; servant of demons, worshiper of the dark one and you must be stopped. They say you can conjure up the minions of the evil one himself and, after what I have personally witnessed lo these many years, I sadly must agree they are right. The pain and misery you have caused, and continue to spew forth cannot continue."

"As you are aware I have personally put to death countless men, women and children in your name, in the glory of the building of your temples, to the splendor of your majesty. Though I am filled with sorrow for what I have done, I have little doubt I will suffer in the fires of Hell for eternity for my actions against these innocents. Now the time has come for these atrocities to stop. You must die, and sadly I, your most humble and trusted servant must be the one to take your life. For only by killing you, can I begin to hope for salvation and forgiveness for the many evils I have committed for your grace. Damn you and damn your heathen temples to Hell."

The uneasy attacker lunged his razor sharp sword at the female body Wilson now possessed but was stopped in mid motion before the blow could make contact. The terrified man stood motionless in lunge position as if paralyzed, frozen in time.

Wilson's female host walked slowly around the paralyzed man as if studying a sculpture in an art museum, taking in all of the nuances of his pose. The overseer's eyes were able to move back and forth, darting sideways, watching his movements. As Wilson completed the circular trip around the man, he felt a growing anger bubbling up inside of this body as if the former indifference the female felt toward this attacker had been replaced with fury. The rage continued to build to greater and greater levels of hatred as if heading for some incredible climatic frenzy.

Wilson felt the shaft begin to pulse in his fingers. Its touch against his palm was as if he were grasping a wooden rod having its exterior covered with living flesh. Looking at the length of the rod, Wilson could see his assumption was dreadfully correct and periodically along the wooden shaft he could see hand-sewn stitches where sections of human flesh had been pieced together to form a literal outer skin for the rod. The site both revolted and yet incredibly intrigued Wilson at the same time. At the top of the fleshy wooden shaft, the blood red eyes of the shining skull had begun to glow and pulse in time with the pulsations Wilson felt from the fleshy shaft.

Wilson heard a now familiar ripping sound as the wall behind the attacker began to split open and once more, long tentacles reached out from the fiery black nothingness waiting beyond the rip in the fabric of the world. A pungent stench of decay poured sickeningly from deep inside the void. The wildly twisting tentacles encompassed his would-be attacker; pulling him toward the opening, while simultaneously melting the flesh from his body. Wilson once again saw the worm-things with their needle-like teeth pouring from the opening and swarming about the screaming man's ankles, working their way upward along his legs, literally devouring his flesh from his body as his muffled screams of torment attempted to pour from his paralytic mouth.

Within a few moments, the half-devoured, half-dissolved man was pulled slowly into the opening. Wilson could hear a cacophony of howling and celebratory shouting coming from within the horrid opening as if the tortured souls of millions of the damned waited to welcome yet another to their fold.

# Chapter 13

Flash .... Wilson was standing in the shadow of a large stone building at sunset, near a rough hand-made plank wooden table upon which a variety of breads and baked goods were stacked. The aromas coming from the food caused Wilson's mouth to water with expectant pleasures. There was still enough sunlight remaining for him to get a good look at his surroundings. He appeared to be in an alley adjacent to some sort of street market which was shutting down at the end of a long business day. He heard some people out in the marketplace speaking in what he thought might be Latin but was uncertain, as he did not speak Latin, yet once again, he could understand their words as clearly, as if they were speaking perfect English.

Examining himself to determine what form he might have now assumed, Wilson saw he was dressed in some type of tattered yellowed tunic. At first he thought perhaps it might be another dress and he might still be in the body of the evil witch woman, but to his relief he realized he had moved on to some other form. He now seemed to be looking through the eyes of a very young man, perhaps an older teenager. His body under the tunic appeared to be slender, perhaps malnourished yet with some developing muscle tone. The ache in his stomach told Wilson this young man had not eaten for quite some time. No wonder he was salivating at the confluence of luscious odors filling the air in the marketplace. He tried to ignore the pangs in his stomach and the sensations in his nostrils because he understood he had important business to conduct first.

Either through intuition or a simple knowledge passed on by the being he now occupied, Wilson realized this boy was a street boy, a orphan who had survived for many years in the alleyways of this and other such Roman towns by sheer will and determination. He knew the young man had found thievery to be his best option for survival and he was hiding in the shadows at this very moment waiting for the opportunity to steal some food, money or both from one of the unsuspecting merchants who was closing down their stand after a long and hopefully prosperous day. He understood also the boy was not above hurting or even killing his victims if that was what it took for him to survive and had done both on more than one occasion in the past.

Looking down Wilson saw he held a dagger in his right hand. He lifted the knife upward to give it a closer examination and he noticed the blade and hilt were shining silver while the handle seemed to be made of some sort of ivory or animal bone, which was inset with two silver skulls with blood red eyes. Apparently, this knife was the boy's main tool for procuring the spoils of his trade. The handle felt almost alive in Wilson's palm and seemed to pulse with the all to familiar rhythm he had experienced earlier with the strange cell phone. He suddenly realized as was the case with the cell phone and the cave man's carved skull and the evil Egyptian queen's scepter, this knife was actually the sacred relic the old man had spoken of, in yet another of its many forms. The knowledge he received from the boy did not explain how he had come to acquire the sacred relic, but he did understand the boy was its present keeper.

Wilson felt a tug as strong hands yanked him backward off his feet pulling him deep into the darkness of the alley behind him. A huge grimy hand covered his mouth and he felt the razor edge of a sharp blade pressed against his throat as a large man spoke into his left ear, "Well what is it we have here? It appears we have a common murdering boy-thief waiting in the shadows to rob and perhaps kill some unsuspecting merchant."

The man's breath was foul, reeking of wine, old cheese and decaying teeth. Wilson could feel the man's wet spittle stippling the side of his face. "I don't take kindly to strangers coming into my neighborhood and robbing the good merchants of this community. These people pay me very well to protect them from common thieves like you, but apparently you did not know that very important fact."

Wilson thought about the modern day extortionists he had learned about by watching his favorite police shows, who coerced store owners to pay them protection money to keep them safe from criminals. Then the merchants soon discover their so-called protectors are the biggest criminals of all. The large man continued, "Well, my foolish young friend, you should have learned to be more careful, for this night you will find you will be the one who will be robbed and murdered."

Wilson heard laughter coming from behind him and the man. It was obvious there were at least two or three more of them back there behind the leader. Therefore, even if he could break free he would likely never escape with his life. The man tightened his grip and Wilson could feel the man was aroused, his maleness poking Wilson's backside through the thin tunic.

"And what a fine specimen of a young man you are. Maybe first, we will want to take some time to get to know you better." The man sneered, poking Wilson a bit more deliberately. The rest of the group all laughed with agreement. Wilson understood at sometime in the past, this young man had suffered the humiliation and savagery of gang rape at the hands of roving packs such as the one which now controlled him, and the boy had sworn to die before permitting such an attack again.

Wilson's arms were pinned helplessly against his sides and he was unable to bring his dagger forward to help him. Being held in this immovable powerless position, frustrated Wilson, and the thought of gang rape angered him beyond understanding as he felt the fury grow inside of him.

"I strongly suggest you drop that lovely blade now my boy." One of the other voices said. "I am certain it will bring us a good deal of money when we sell it, that is. I think after we each get our turn with you we will enjoy gutting you with it." He heard more laughter coming from the darkness. This obvious ridicule brought on new levels of rage and humiliation. Wilson was certain this young thief was about to experience his last few moments on the earth which would be marked by his rape and murder at the hands of this pack of roving tormentors. Instead of feeling fear, he was sharing the boy's anger and could feel the fury growing greater with ever moment.

Wilson did not obey the command to drop the knife, but instead gripped the handle of his dagger even more firmly and felt the skulls beating rhythmically beneath his grasp. He imagined the eyes glowing bright crimson as he allowed all of his rage to flow into the dagger.

From the darkness behind him, he heard a ripping sound and closed his eyes knowing very well the incredible horrors that would soon follow. Suddenly all around him amid the stench of death he heard the agonizing screams of his would-be attackers. The knife at his throat fell harmlessly to the ground, the huge man's body fell backward away from him as he stood rigid, eyes squeezed tightly shut, all the while smelling burning flesh and boiling blood while hearing the wild and uncontrolled thrashing of horror occurring behind him. Then he heard the skittering of hundreds of spider-like feet along the cobblestone street as his attackers were dragged screaming and howling helplessly back into the darkness.

# Chapter 14

Flash.... Wilson found himself sitting at a round wooden table in a dimly lit back room of an old wood-framed building. Sunlight from the outside shown through the cracks in the wood-planked walls. The smell of beer, whiskey, cigar smoke, human sweat and body odor filled the air. The table was covered with money, playing cards and empty whiskey glasses.

Across the table from him sat a tall rough-looking man with a pockmarked face, a dark full mustache, at least two days worth of beard stubble. Greasy black hair hung long under the shade of his dusty black leather cowboy hat. A cigar stub hung from the man's mouth as smoke climbed skyward causing the man's eyes to remain slightly closed, to avoid the fumes, giving him a Clint Eastwood, squinty appearance. Wilson felt as if he were sitting in a saloon scene in one of his favorite Sergio Leone's spaghetti westerns. However, this was not a movie; this was the real deal. The man's expression was one of utter contempt as he sat tensed, ready to strike, holding an antique looking six-gun pointed directly at Wilson's face.

Likewise, three other similar looking characters seated around the table were pointing their guns at him, all waiting for the signal from cigar man to splatter Wilson's guts and brains all over the back wall. Wilson looked down at the table and saw he too had his hand on top of what must be his own gun lying atop the table. He apparently was not able to reach it fast enough to outdraw the group.

He saw his gun was a silver colored beauty with a pearl handle. Inlaid in the handle of the gun visible just under his palm was a silver skull with two blood red eyes. The skull's eyes reflected light from the oil lamps hanging on the wall. The air was thick with cigar smoke, which seemed more like a glaring fog as it was illuminated by the filtering sunlight.

The angry man across the table from Wilson said over the barrel of his gun, "Not so fast there, partner." Wilson could not believe this character actually said the word 'partner', just like in an old Western movie. Normally this would be too strange and perhaps too corny for him to consider taking seriously. However, the looks of anger on the men's faces and the muzzles of their guns all pointed directly at him, told Wilson he had better put aside his opinions for now and try to find a way out of this mess.

The man continued. "I don't know what you may have gotten away with at your last stopover, stranger, but in my town when someone gets caught cheating at cards, then tries to go for his gun, we usually make sure he ends up with a belly full of lead." There it was again, Wilson wondered. Stranger? Belly full of lead? This was all starting to feel a bit like a bad attempt to lampoon the western genre, but again, despite his criticism, the apparent danger was all too real.

Understanding the seriousness of the situation, the body Wilson now occupied was allowing his anger at these men to build and Wilson understood why. He could feel the hatred growing like a power generator winding up for a major surge. After what he had been through so far on this eventful night Wilson knew completely well what was going to happen next and strangely, instead of feeling horror or loathing at what was to come, he began to anticipate it with pleasure to look forward to it. There would be no death for him this night at the hand of these men, for in his hand he held the relic and in his heart was great hatred and anger and by allowing this anger to build to an uncontrollable fury he would be saved. Wilson was finding the power present in the relic to be more intoxicating than his favorite liquor.

Wilson could feel the gun begin to throb and pulse under his palm as the ripping sound came from the middle of the air high above them. His attackers barely had time to look upward to check on the strange noise when dozens of long burning tentacles dropped from above, dangling like the legs of an octopus from the air. They instantly wrapped themselves around the gun-hands of the men, severing their arms at the wrist with their molten hot grasps. Not all of the severed wrists were cauterized instantly and pools of flowing blood pumped onto the table.

The horrid worms with the needle-like teeth fell to the tabletop and began scurrying in all directions; some greedily began drinking up the puddles of warm rich blood while others were busy latching onto the first pieces of living flesh they could find. The spider-like creatures scampered down the arms of the flopping tentacles jumping onto the faces of the screaming men, devouring their flesh as the men howled in agony. Wilson saw the leader with the cigar still hanging from his mouth; his eyes wide with horror sitting helplessly paralyzed as the human-headed spider creatures systematically consumed his face. Out from the flaming tip of his cigar, poked the head of one of the worm creatures, looking about, opening its needle-filled mouth whining a high-pitched cry of pleasure.

One of the men fell face down on the table as his scalp literally fell off in a sickening red flap, exposing his now steaming white skull. In a few seconds, Wilson could see a series of small boreholes appearing about the surface of the skull, each gradually growing larger. Soon the holes were the size of a quarter, as gelatinous gray matter began to ooze from the openings, dripping the sludge down onto the table. Mixed in with the brain matter, thousands of steaming writhing maggots all feasted on the mess.

Wilson could hear the men's bones begin to rattle like some sort of gigantic wind chime from Hell as his attackers, now just dead carcasses, barely covered with flesh were pulled upward into the black and flaming void above. Again, Wilson could hear the cries of millions of lost souls howling from the inside of the chasm, which seamed itself shut as the air above the table returned to normal. Wilson, stood, no longer upset or overwhelmed by the horrors and reached across the table gathering up all of the gambling money, placing his special six-gun in his holster and heading out the back door of the saloon.

These scenes countless others even more horrible, spanning centuries of time played and replayed repeatedly during the night, bombarding Wilson's mind through his dreams like some sort of twisted educational video. By the time morning arrived Wilson would have a thorough understanding of just what this phone was, and what it could do for him.

# Chapter 15

Charles Wilson awoke to the sound of a phone ringing. At first the ringing sounded as if he were hearing it far away in the distance, or from deep down in a well, far below the surface of the earth. The volume of the sound steadily increased until he was awake enough to realize what the sound was, the hotel phone waiting to be answered.

As he slowly reached consciousness, in a state of disorientation, he found himself sprawled on his back on top of his bedspread, staring straight up at the ceiling, drenched in sweat from head to toe. He lifted himself up onto his elbows in a half sitting position, his muscles aching and realized he was unable to move the lower part of his body.

He soon discovered his legs were still hanging down over the bottom edge of the bed where they apparently had hung since last evening when he had collapsed into unconsciousness. He tried to move to answer the phone only to find his legs had fallen asleep and felt like two dead weights attached to the bottom half of his body. The phone continued to ring incessantly. He forced himself into a clumsy sort of roll, dragging his dead slumbering legs along with him and somehow managed to reach the bedside table to answer the phone.

"Hello?" Wilson said in a raspy voice, still thick with sleep.

"This is your six a-m wake up call. Have a wonderful day." Wilson heard the computerized robotic voice announcing through the headset.

"Wake this!" Wilson said in frustration, slamming down the receiver, still trying to shake off the confusion of the night's sleep. Apparently, the effects of the whiskey were still clouding his thoughts because he did not immediately recall any of the incredible events of the previous night or the horrible dreams that followed. For the moment, he was having enough trouble simply regaining consciousness. He felt like someone thirty feet under water, trying desperately to reach the sunlit surface but slowly progressing upward through water thick as soup.

The feeling was gradually starting to return to legs in the form of a thousand prickling needles tingling painfully within his muscles. He stumbled to his feet hoping to get some blood circulating into his stinging limbs, grimacing from the unpleasant sensation. He positioned himself next to the bed half standing, resting one arm on the end table just in case his legs decided to give out on him. He could feel the blood flowing back down into his waking legs and could sense the strength slowly returning to them.

The television at the foot of the bed was still on. Wilson realized he must have passed out without turning it off last night. He looked at the television from across the room through still bleary eyes trying desperately to focus, and saw the national morning news was airing. He stood in his half-bent position as the feeling was now rapidly returning to his legs. Then abruptly, Wilson was shocked back to reality as he saw the news was replaying the video from last evening of Randal Lee Forester falling into the crack in the earth.

Suddenly, the television seemed to fly away from him as if he was flying backward at incredible speed through a long tunnel as the floodgates opened in his mind and, everything came rushing back. He recalled every single moment, real or imagined, of the previous night and every detail of every horrible nightmare he had experienced; the store, the old man, the robber, the phone, the opening of the portal, the fiery tentacles, the needle toothed worms and spiders with human faces.

He stumbled backward, sitting on the bed where he remained trembling, trying to get himself under control. He lowered his head into his hands hoping his mind would start to clear soon. He looked down at the bed cover, wet with sweat, where he had spent the night and lying next to the darkened shape, he saw the blood red cell phone. It seemed to mock him in its silence.

Wilson jumped off the bed as if he had just seen a rat crawling on the bed cover, trying desperately to distance himself from the accursed thing. For a moment, he thought his legs might not hold him as the room began to spiral around him. He staggered clumsily to the bathroom falling to his knees in front of the toilet and vomiting as he had never vomited before, almost as if his body was attempting to cleanse itself of the contaminating filth, as the body purges itself during an illness or from food poisoning.

He held onto the sides of the bowl, retching, dry heaving and trembling uncontrollably, arms shaking, knees wobbling. When the tremors finally subsided and the retching ceased, Wilson flushed the toiled, pulled down the lid and lay his head on top of the cover, breathing rapidly, arms dangling by the sides of the toilet. He honestly thought he was going do die right where he was, that perhaps his heart would simply stop or his body would just shut down from exhaustion.

When he thought he might once again be able to stand he cautiously got to his feet, went to the sink, turned on the light, which temporarily blinded him with its florescent glow, then vigorously began brushing his teeth. He brushed, rinsed and spat repeatedly trying to get the foul taste from his mouth and nostrils. Slowly as his eyes adjusted, he looked up into the bathroom mirror.

The figure looking back at him was startling to say the least. Wilson appeared to have aged ten years overnight. He had always had a thick head of hair with a distinguished looking salt a pepper appearance, just a touch of gray at the temples. However, now he thought he was slightly grayer then the night before, and the laugh lines and eye wrinkles on his face seem to have doubled over the course of one evening. Perhaps it was simply his imagination, but judging by how poorly he felt he was unsure.

Wilson pushed his disheveled hair back from his eyes and thought just for a moment maybe his hair was starting to recede more than normal. He always watched his hairline as was both proud and somewhat vain about his thick head of hair. He also thought he noticed a slightly darker tan patch of skin at his hairline. What was that, an age spot? He looked at the backs of his hands which also appeared a bit more wrinkled and thought he saw a few age spots forming there as well. He was only forty-five years old for God's sake, and did not expect to see this sort of thing for at least ten more years.

Wilson looked up to see the four-foot florescent light fixture hanging above the mirror and felt little a bit better about things. Yes, that must have been the problem. He recalled how florescent lighting tended to make everyone look worse, especially first thing in the morning. Considering he had just barfed his guts out, how good could he possibly look? He also took into consideration the eventful evening he had, but still he preferred to blame at least some of it on the lighting. He knew the best thing for him to do immediately, was to freshen up with a good long hot shower.

Charles Wilson was one of those people who seemed to react to hot showers in a very positive way. Not just because it cleansed and refreshed him, but because there was something so invigorating about a steaming hot shower that it seemed to stimulate his creative juices. He always got his best and most imaginative ideas while taking a shower. He had no idea why this happened but understood it and accepted it just did.

Since the nature of Wilson's job was such that he wasn't required to punch a clock and wasn't tied to a desk he spent most of his time visiting clients throughout the workweek. This freedom gave him the luxury of being able to schedule his own time. Often during the day if he found he was having trouble focusing, was in a funk, or could not seem to come up with original ways to bring in new business, he would stop home, between appointments and take a steaming shower and the ideas would flow out of his mind as the water flowed around him. It might sound a bit odd to many people but Charles understood what worked for him and a hot shower was just the thing to get his mind working.

Wilson stood under the streaming hot water feeling all of the stress flowing from his body and exiting down the drain. As he sensed the water, coursing down his back and smelled the fresh shampoo and steam billowing around him he began to recount the dreams, which had visited him during the night. In his relaxed condition, Wilson was surprised to find the dreams no longer troubled him, as things of such a horrific nature should have, but he felt like the dreams were things he needed to consider, to analyze, and to understand. He obviously had the dreams for a purpose and he had to find out what that purpose might be.

When he thought back to each dream, how he was part of each dream, he at first believed he was seeing these dreams as some sort of reincarnation; perhaps the people in his dreams were supposed to be various incarnations of himself. Then he realized this idea was not correct, he was not actually the cave man or any of the other principals in the dreams but was simply seeing through their eyes. Perhaps this format was used so he could more easily be taught what he needed to learn.

He believed the events he witnessed in his dreams were not symbolic representations but were actual events which had happened to those specific people throughout history. Somehow, the relic had come into their possession and had affected their lives. Why these people were chosen or why he, himself was chosen he still did not yet understand but knew there was a definite reason why he was allowed to view these images during his dreams.

Wilson thought perhaps he was shown these events so he could learn about the relic, which was now in the form of a cell phone lying on his bedspread in the other room. He realized the dreams may have been presented as some form of remote viewing, so he could understand exactly how long the relic had existed, and what it might be able to do for him.

Wilson was amazed at how, while under the shower, he could be so relaxed he could systematically consider all of the events of the night before whereas otherwise he feared reliving the events might have driven him completely insane. For a moment, Wilson wondered if perhaps the trauma he suffered actually had broken his mind and maybe he was crazy after all. He didn't think he was, but how many crazy people did? Oddly, the notion did not seem to matter to him, for either way, sane or insane, Charles Wilson understood everything about him had changed forever.

Then as often happened during special times like this, Wilson had an epiphany. He realized the dreams truly were not nightmares or things to be feared; they were there to help him learn. He had a brief image of training videos, which he watched at work. Yes, like training videos, these dreams were meant to teach him, to orient him into a new phase of his life, help him to transition to a new level. He was beginning to have some sort of awakening, and it made him feel very good inside.

Wilson understood this phone, this 'relic' could be used to benefit him greatly. If he learned not to fear it but to use it, he realized he could indeed become a very wealthy and powerful man. Suddenly Wilson felt as if he had been filled with knowledge, as if he had been transformed into a new Charles Wilson, a more powerful Charles Wilson, and a Charles Wilson who could do anything he chose. He was amazed at how his confidence had grown with the realization he now had a fantastic power he could use however he wished. He was not just the keeper of the phone; he was the master of the phone.

Wilson stepped out of the shower a changed man. As the steam from his shower dissipated though the open bathroom door, Charles Wilson took another look at himself in the mirror and decided not only had he not aged during the night but he looked better and stronger than ever. He felt like he could take on the world and that was exactly what he planned to do, and woe be to any man who tried to get in his way.

# Chapter 16

At 8:50 am Charles Wilson arrived at the offices of Harcourt and Washington, for one of the most important meetings of his career. The building, which housed the firm, soared over fifty stories into the morning sky, a massive structure of brick, chrome and glass; prime real estate for only the most influential and prosperous of companies.

Interestingly, this morning Wilson did not feel any negative effects from his previous evening's ordeal, nor was he nervous or anxious about this final meeting to sign his contract paperwork. If the old Charles Wilson had been a self-assured hard-nosed businessman, this new Charles Wilson was that to the tenth power. He was a man of complete confidence, a man in charge; he was the man who made things happen.

The cell phone which had terrified him so much the previous night, now was sitting comfortably in the inside pocket of his suit jacket positioned directly over his heart. Having the phone with its unearthly pulse so close to his this vital life-giving organ, now made him feel quite good, made him feel like nothing could go wrong. From time to time, the phone almost seemed to squirm against his chest, as if attempting to crawl closer to him, crawl into him. Yesterday, such a sensation would have made Wilson cringe with disgust. However, this motion no longer bothered Wilson in the least; it now made him feel content to know the phone, the sacred relic was close by.

Wilson noticed a newspaper stand on the corner as he approached the building. A headline screamed the question, 'Divine Retribution?' in bold print across the front page. Wilson knew this would most certainly be a story about the death of Randal Lee Forester outside of the Yuengsville courthouse late last evening. He paid little attention to the headline and had no need to read the story, because he created the story. In fact, he was the story. It was simply no one else in the world knew about his involvement, or ever would, which was just fine with him. This made Wilson laugh to himself. That disgusting slime ball Forester was probably just beginning to sample just a few of the tortures Hell had to offer him and which he would be experiencing for eternity. Wilson wished there was a way for the phone to show him how Forester was suffering. Someday he would have to try to figure out if it would be possible.

For now, Wilson decided to put his personal pleasure aside and focus on the events at hand. During the past year, he had been negotiating a deal, more like a mega-deal, with R. John Showalter, the Executive Vice President of H & W. The multi-million dollar deal, once signed, would contract Wilson's company to design and implement a new data management system for every one of H & W's fifty-seven worldwide locations.

Showalter was third man from the top at Harcourt and Washington, with Johnson P. Harcourt being the top man and Samuel F. Washington being the second from the top. Both top men were sons of the original founders of the company. Even after two solid and profitable years with the company, Showalter was still considered somewhat of an outsider by the two leaders, his not being a family member. And, as is often typical with family run companies and partnerships, Showalter had reached the highest position a non-family member could possibly reach at H & W. Although he felt secure in his position, he was aware Johnson P. Harcourt's oldest son Johnson P Harcourt III, was a freshman in college and someday would be coming on board, in a created top position, essentially dropping Showalter down a notch on the totem pole to fourth from the top. Wilson suspected this fact did not sit very well with Showalter and perhaps would be the reason someday soon John might leave H & W. Charles wanted to be sure he managed to squeeze all of the deals out of Showalter long before that occurred.

Wilson knew since the deal he was working with Showalter would total in the millions, his own personal commission would be so large it might be considered obscene. Yes, he would be sitting pretty, not to mention the promotion and salary bump, which would surly follow. Wilson had already been planning how he would spend all of the money. In fact, he had already spent a large portion of his pending commission on a new car, a big screen television and surround sound setup. Since he and his wife had never had and children he was assured, waiting in his future would be a good number of vacations to exotic locations as well.

Wilson approached the security desk in the lobby of the building to announce he was there for a nine o'clock meeting with Mr. Showalter in the Harcourt and Washington offices. Wilson had gone through this required ritual many times in the past year and actually knew most of the security guards by name.

"Morning Jim," Wilson said cheerfully, "I am heading up to H & W to finalize this deal I have been working on with them. "

"That's great news Mr. Wil.." the guard said, stopping in mid sentence. Wilson saw the guard staring at him with a horrified expression as if he had seen the Satan himself. The guard blinked once as if trying to refocus his vision, then regained his composure before his face flushed red with embarrassment. "I'm terribly sorry, Mr. Wilson, must be the lighting in here. It made you look different somehow, I though I saw somethin... I mean someone else."

Wilson wondered what exactly it was the man had seen. Was there something about his physical appearance that had changed? Charles knew he had forever changed on the inside; but perhaps there was something about him people saw differently on the outside as well. He did not know if it would be a good thing or not, judging by the horrified expression the guard had shown, perhaps it was not a good thing at all.

Had he been able to see what the guard had seen, he would have understood the reason for the man's terror. The guard had looked up expecting to see the genial face of Charles Wilson and saw much more than he bargained for. It was as if Wilson's outer pleasant face was some type of clear transparent mask with Charles' face painted upon it. But, just below the clear mask was another face, ancient, wretched and horrible swirling just under the surface of his skin. To the guard it appeared as if the face were comprised of worms and maggots all moving over, under and around each other in a cacophony of motion, all trying equally to burst out and bore their way to the surface. Then, just as quickly the image faded and Wilson's face had returned to normal, causing great trepidation and embarrassment for the man.

Wanting to put it all behind him, the security guard clumsily handed Wilson his access badge, asked him to sign into the guest book then directed him to take the appropriate elevator, which would take him straight to the executive offices of H and W on the 45$^{th}$ floor of the building. Wilson noticed the man never looked directly at his face again during the exchange, as if doing so, the man would risk seeing whatever it was he saw earlier which terrified him. As the elevator doors closed Wilson saw the guard staring at him peculiarly as the man picked up the phone to announce Wilson's arrival to Showalter's secretary.

Wilson left the elevator on the 45$^{th}$ floor heading directly to the receptionist's desk. "Good morning Jennifer." Wilson said cheerfully, having become equally familiar with the woman during the past year as well. She did not offer her usual smile or offer any other pleasantries; instead, she simply gave a curt "'Morning. Mr. Wilson." As with Jim the security guard, Jennifer chose not to look directly at him and continued with strange detachment, "Mr. Showalter is waiting in his office and would like to see you immediately."

Wilson thought this was odd as well, since Jennifer was generally very friendly and happy to see him. However, today her attitude toward him was very strange indeed. He wondered if Jim the security guard had called her and said something about the 'difference' he had seen in Wilson, warning her not to look directly at him. Perhaps Charles was simply being paranoid. Or, maybe Jennifer had some sort of sixth sense, a women's intuition, and somehow tuned into the difference in Wilson, sensing his vibrations and not liking what she felt. He did not know what her problem was, nor did he really care. He was here to close a deal and after today, he suspected his visits to H & W would be much less frequent. He proceeded in to see his client as Jennifer had instructed.

As Wilson entered Showalter's office, he instantly felt something was not right. Showalter approached him shaking his hand half-heartedly and couldn't seem to make eye contact with him either. But Wilson suspected his lack of eye contact was for a completely different reason than the guards and receptionist's. Wilson sensed Showalter was averting his eyes because the man was about to deliver some very bad news to him.

"I tried to call you several times yesterday afternoon but your cell constantly went to voice mail," Showalter said in an annoying, frustrated tone, still opting not to make eye contact with Wilson.

Wilson attempted to explain, "Well John, I am quite embarrassed to say in my haste to catch my plane yesterday, I left my business cell at home. I have never done anything like that before and I honestly don't understand how it could have happened. I cannot believe I did such a stupid thing and I am terribly sorry about everything."

"Well, it was extremely unfortunate." Showalter continued in his icy tone. "It was critical I reach you yesterday. As I have mentioned in the past, when you deal with Harcourt and Washington, you need to be available twenty-four seven."

Wilson apologized again, frustrated and becoming angry because he, with is new found amazing powers still had to lower himself to groveling to such a lowly human, "As I said, John, this was an accident; a one-time thing. I am never without my cell phone. I have always been available to you and your company any time and any place, including when I was on vacation, as you may recall."

Showalter interrupted Wilson, "So you have told me, Charles. And I will admit this has been the case all throughout this decision making process, but the fact remains you were not available yesterday late in the day when we needed to speak to you; and as you should very well know, in business, timing is everything."

Wilson was becoming angrier by the minute. Who did this Showalter, think he was, treating him like a child. If this man knew the power Charles had within his grasp, he would be on his knees begging for his life. Still choosing to play the role of businessman, Charles tempered his comments somewhat saying, "I don't understand what you are inferring John, surely one little misplaced cell phone at this late date in our negotiations, cannot be that critical." Wilson inquired.

"Normally it would be the case," Showalter continued, "Normally, whatever we had to discuss could have waited until this morning, but were are down to the wire on this, Charles. Remember I am supposed to commit H & W to a multi-million-dollar deal with your company. I would think as the main representative of Edmondson Systems, you would have gone out of your way to make yourself available. And more importantly, Mr. Harcourt and Mr. Washington would have thought so as well."

# Chapter 17

Wilson instantly understood now they were
getting to the main crux of this little cat and mouse
game, that being Johnson P. Harcourt, himself.
Wilson began to comprehend perhaps his 'done
deal' might have just taken a bad turn, with the
main man in the corporation now involved. Wilson
had very little use for J. P. Harcourt, feeling the
man had grown up privileged; born with a silver
spoon in his mouth. Charles felt Harcourt the
company was given to J. P. without his having to lift
a finger to work for it. As a result, Wilson thought
the man was as dumber than a stump, to put it not
so politely. He knew John Showalter was the real
brains of the corporation, while J. P. Harcourt and
Samuel Washington were mere figureheads; spoiled
rich boys, the both of them.

However, one fact remained the same; their
names were on the company letterhead and they
paid the salaries, including Showalter's. Moreover,
that meant Wilson had to walk a fine line in these
negotiations, at least until he could get a feel for the
situation. He was fully aware Showalter would only
stick his neck out so far for him.

Wilson asked curiously, "Mr. Harcourt? I am surprised to hear he would want to be involved in these discussions, especially at this late stage in the process. I was of the impression this was your project and you were the final decision maker on it. I don't understand why the busy president of a global company such as H & W would want to take the time to put his stamp on this."

Showalter continued his explanation, "Traditionally he would not do so. He generally hands this sort of project over to me and allows me make all the final decisions. However, as you are aware, this is an enormous venture, involving a great investment on our part and which affects literally every facility we own worldwide; not to mention the fact that the final implementation will take two years to complete. I suppose Mr. Harcourt felt he needed to be involved at this final hour, just to help him feel shall we say 'warm and fuzzy'."

"Charles, as I hope you are aware for the past year I have been talking your company up, and putting my name, not to mention my neck, on the line for you, Mr. Edmondson and Edmondson Systems. What you may not know is Mr. Harcourt had some other companies in mind which he actually preferred to use."

For some reason, the revelation caught Wilson completely by surprise. Up until that very moment, he had believed Edmondson Systems was the only viable player in the game. Certainly, there were other competitors capable of doing the job, but none with the prestige and reputation his company had, and none had put so much time, energy and work into making the deal a reality as he had done. Perhaps he had been too sure, too confident all along, not taking into account the political climate surrounding the project. He should have realized 'rich boy' Harcourt would have one of his old cronies waiting in the wings to jump in at the final hour and steal his lunch.

Showalter continued, "It became an extremely politically sensitive situation around here. The smart thing for me to have done was to just go along with Harcourt, sign the other company right away and leave you out in the cold. Nevertheless, I really believed Edmondson Systems was the right fit for this project.

What you do not realize is all during this time I have stuck to my convictions and told Harcourt you were the right company for the job. That was a great professional risk on my part if things did not work out the way H & W wanted them to. Mr. Harcourt as much as said my job was on the line, if this project failed."

"I truly appreciate it John." Wilson said, genuinely grateful for what Showalter must have gone through, but still very concerned about what he, Charles, might have to do in order to win this project. He needed to come up with an alternate plan.

Wilson realized although he appeared to have an ally in Showalter, the man had gone about as far as he chose to in order to help support Wilson. And, from this point on it would take all of Wilson's business sense and negotiating skills to keep the deal on the table; and he was certain, more than a little help from some powers not of this earth.

"So..." Showalter interrupted, "Yesterday I got a call from Mr. Harcourt telling me he wanted to speak to you personally and had some last minute questions. I tried to argue with him and say everything was fine, but he insisted; and since he is the one who signs my paycheck, I gave him your cell phone number. And of course he could not reach you."

Charles wonder to himself, "And how strangely convenient was that?" The one time J. P. Harcourt needed urgently to speak to him was the one time he did not happen to have his cell phone available. There were definitely some strange forces at odds around this deal and Charles was right in the thick of things. He began to formulate a plan, or at least what he hoped would become a plan offering a solution, albeit a 'final solution' to the situation.

"He tried many times to reach you, as did I before finally giving up." Showalter said. "He even called your boss Mr. Edmondson, and ordered him to find a way to get in touch with you."

Wilson almost laughed aloud at the thought of T. Martin Edmondson on the phone, ordered around by that idiot Harcourt. The old man must have been on the verge of an aneurysm. The entire situation was beginning to amuse Wilson. With his new powerful legions of the damned, he found he could look at things from a completely different perspective. He was above worrying about ridiculous human drivel and petty political stupidity. In his pocket he had the ability to manipulate and control destiny.

"Yes." Wilson said, pretending to sound genuinely contrite, "Late last evening when I called my wife she mentioned Mr. Edmondson was trying to get in touch with me, but it was very late, I was exhausted and figured I would simply call him after our meeting."

"That was rather unfortunate." Showalter reprimanded, "Needless to say, I took a lot of heat for it. And because of the unfortunate mix-up, Mr. Harcourt started to second guess me and question again if I had made the right decision in going with your company."

Charles could tell by Showalter's body actions and tone of voice the man was getting ready to throw Wilson 'under the bus' so to speak. Showalter might be willing to stick his neck out a bit, but not so far, that Harcourt would be waiting to chop it off like a Thanksgiving turkey.

His anger growing, Wilson questioned. "Are you saying Harcourt told you not to use our company based simply on my not being available on my personal cell phone on a Sunday afternoon? Are you saying he plans to throw away all of our hard work and preparation for something so trivial, as meaningless as this?" Wilson could feel the cell phone starting to vibrate in his suit pocket.

Showalter continued, appearing to be back peddling. "Well, at that time, he did still leave the final decision up to me, but he made his displeasure perfectly clear. Charles, he chewed my ass out at home on my supposed Sunday afternoon off while at the same time trying to persuade me to see things his way and abandon our deal. As I said, even though he runs the show he does prefer to have his subordinates make up our own minds; or so I thought until this morning."

"Ah," Wilson thought to himself. "Here it comes. This will be the place, where Showalter buckles under pressure and abandons ship." He imagined a sinking ship with hundreds of rats jumping off into the ocean. This will be where Wilson would find himself alone, adrift in a vast empty sea, abandoned without a life raft or another rescue ship in sight.

His plan was starting to take shape now, but he needed to gather a bit more information first. "Well then, what happened this morning?" Wilson insisted, his frustration and anger visibly growing.

"Well," Showalter hesitantly said, "Mr. Harcourt came storming into the building like a mad man heading straight for my office, scaring my secretary half to death. Bottom line Wilson is he has insisted, in fact he has ordered me not to sign the deal with your company under any circumstances, and to go with a competitor instead. You know if decision were still mine to make, I would give the contract to your company, but this is no longer the case. It is no longer up to me; it is up to Mr.

Harcourt. And he will not permit any contract to be signed with Edmondson Systems."

Wham! Pow! There it was; right in the kisser! Wilson felt as if he had been hit across the face with a baseball bat. There was no way he would let this deal fall through. He no longer cared about the commission, the potential promotion, his reputation. Now it was a matter of personal principal. He had worked his ass off for this deal for a year and no way would a moron like Harcourt stop him from getting what was rightfully his.

He anger began to boil. Wilson said sternly, "John...John...listen to me. You can't let that idiot Harcourt screw up this deal. I know you are the real brains behind this company and you actually run it. Harcourt is a fool and Washington is a simpleton. You know how hard we both worked for this. You need to be a man, to step up, take charge, and tell Harcourt you demand he go with our company. If you insist, I know he will back down, unless he is actually so incredibly stupid that he is not aware of how much he needs you."

Showalter insisted. "I'm sorry Charles. I really want to help you. However, Mr. Harcourt told me directly if I attempted to sign with your company and legally committed H & W to this contract, I would be on the street looking for a new job by noon. In addition, he would tie the deal up in legal red tape for years. That would not benefit either of us. The bottom line is Charles, I simply can't do this deal with you."

The cell phone began to pulse more agitatedly inside his jacket as Wilson's fury continued to grow. Wilson said through gritted teeth, "Very well then John... just please.. Answer one simple... question for me. Have you actually signed with anyone else yet... you know.... Have you physically signed another contract?"

Appearing somewhat confused, Showalter said, "Well, no I have not... Not yet. But Bill

Simpson, whom I assume know, from Ultra Tech will be arriving at 11:00 am this morning for me to sign his contract."

"Ultra Tech?" Wilson thought. "Bill Simpson? Yes that would explain a lot." Charles knew Simpson and Harcourt were old time buddies since back in their early college days; probably frat brothers or some other such nonsense. And although under normal circumstances, Ultra Tech wouldn't have a chance at getting a deal this big, there appeared to be forces at hand turning the tide in their favor; perhaps not unearthly or demonic forces, but maybe something equally as powerful and equally as evil; political forces and the forces of cronyism. However, what these fools did not realize was Wilson had an ace in his pocket, literally, and within a instant he saw his entire strategy laid out in his mind. He had his plan and it was time to make it a reality.

Wilson suggested, "Then there is still time."

"What the Hell are you talking about Wilson?" Showalter asked. "There is no time. There is no more deal. It's over. It's done."

Wilson demanded, "Tell me John, who besides you, myself and Harcourt is aware of his decision to break this deal?" He noticed a bit of resistance on the part of Showalter to answer and asked again, "John, this is very important to me." John Showalter looked Wilson in the eyes appearing to be uncertain if he should tell him or not then finally seeming to agree perhaps, Charles had a right to the information he requested.

"Well." Showalter said, appearing to do so with great reluctance, "Other than Mr. Harcourt, I suppose Mr. Washington must know by now, since the both of them are having a private meeting down the hall at this very moment in Mr. Harcourt's office."

That was exactly what Charles Wilson needed to hear. He knew now what he had to do next. "Well then." Wilson insisted, "All is not lost after all."

Showalter looked at Wilson as if he was looking at a crazy man. As he watched, Wilson started to behave very strangely, placing his right palm against his heart, closing his eyes and putting his head down slightly as if concentrating greatly. Showalter looked as if he thought perhaps the stress of the meeting had been too much for Wilson and the man might be having a heart attack.

Showalter questioned sympathetically, "Wilson? Charles? Are you all right? Should I get help for you?"

Wilson held up his left hand in a stop gesture and Showalter flew backward pressed tightly against the back of the chair, the leather upholstery of the chair crushed inward from the mounting pressure, his arms dangling at his side, unable to move or speak as he watched Wilson in his rising concentration.

Next, Wilson looked directly into Showalter's terrified eyes, smiled a sinister smile and calmly said, "There is something I want you to see. Something you must see."

# Chapter 18

An instant later, John Showalter miraculously found himself in the office of Johnson P. Harcourt floating high above the man close to the ceiling. The sensation was like those descriptions of out of body experiences often depicted on television shows. He could see and hear everything going on below him, though he was invisible to the parties below. He looked to his left and sensed the presence of another phantom, similar to himself, and saw a translucent image of Charles Wilson, wearing a sinister smile, suspended in the air next to him. J. P. Harcourt was sitting behind his massive desk, hands folded in a tepee shape, agitatedly discussing his displeasure with Showalter and Wilson and the entire Edmondson Systems situation.

"Sam," Harcourt said, "I know you are somewhat fond of Showalter, actually much more fond of him than I am, but I think after this Edmondson debacle we have to consider letting him go."

Washington looked shocked at the suggestion. "Debacle? Letting him go? Are you serious J. P.?" Washing asked, "John Showalter has been an exceptional employee since we brought him on board. He has been single-handedly responsible for making us a ton of money as well."

"Perhaps so." Harcourt said. "And in all fairness, he has, in turn been well compensated for his work, as we both know. But there is something about this man that makes me very uncomfortable, something underhanded about his actions. He is much too ambitious for my taste. He has only been with us for just under two years and he had managed to insert himself into every aspect of running this company. If something every happened to either of us, Showalter could simply take over with the board of director's approval and run the place flawlessly, as if it were his own company."

"But isn't that a good thing?" Washington countered. "His hard work, ambition and desire to run things, allows us to take more time to enjoy ourselves and to do the things we find relaxing, while still making tons of money. That sounds like a win-win situation to me."

Harcourt said. "But Samuel. This company is ours; our families' not his. It was formed as a partnership between your father and mine. And although you have no children interested in pursuing the business, I do, and I don't want an interloper like Showalter doing anything to undermine my current authority or my son's future authority."

Showalter watched from above; the anger seething within him. Harcourt continued. "Besides, in my opinion, he dropped the ball big-time on this one. That Wilson character and his fly-by-night company, Edmondson systems, somehow has pulled the wool over his eyes, and as a result he almost signed a multi-million dollar contract with them." Harcourt continued, "Thank goodness I had the wisdom and forethought to intervene and stop this fiasco at the last minute before it became a legal nightmare."

Washington, who was always the most indecisive of the pair, began to waffle and give in to Harcourt's demands, as he always seemed to do. "Well, I don't know J. P. Although I am not really in favor of it, I suppose if you feel so strongly it is what is best for the future of our company then perhaps it is what we must do."

"Those bastards!" Showalter said in the form of a thought wave which seemed to pass from his mind to Wilson's, from his invisible floating observatory. "They can't do this to me."

Washington continued. "But since it is your idea, I would prefer you take care of notifying him, and I am more than willing to offer him a nice compensation package. After all, there is no call for us to put him out in the street without a suitable severance package."

Harcourt said. "I will take care of it. I can have the papers drawn up in accordance with his contract as soon as this meeting is over, then I will go to the board of directors with my recommendation, or should I say demand, and I am certain they will back me up on the decision."

"So the board doesn't know about it yet?" Washington questioned.

Harcourt offered, "Of course not Samuel. I would never take any such action without clearing it with my partner first. So far, you and I are the only ones who know about this."

Deep inside of his mind, Showalter heard Charles Wilson say, "As you can see John, they can and they most definitely will not hesitate to toss you out into the street in a single ticking beat of your heart. As I said, you are the brains of this company and even those two morons know that, yet they are willing to throw you to the wolves without a second thought."

"There must be something you can do to stop this. If you can accomplish this strange out of body thing, while I am actually sitting down the hall pressed against my desk chair, then there must be something you can do to help me. Is there Charles?" Showalter seemed to plead.

Wilson explained, "Of course there is John. But first I need to know we are a team, that when I am finished, no matter what you may see happen here today, we will still have a deal."

"As far as I am concerned, I will sign the contract in blood if necessary, Charles." Showalter said, "Just do what you have to do to rid me of these two fools."

"Well then, John." Wilson said, "Just sit back, relax and enjoy the show while your new partner puts and end to all of this ridiculous nonsense."

Down below the floating phantoms, J. P. Harcourt and Samuel Wilson both heard a loud ripping sound, as the air behind Harcourt's desk seemed to shimmer and ripple for a few seconds, just before an enormous split began to form in the middle of the air. This opening started as a small black tear in the atmosphere, then opened to a larger rip about three feet off the ground; its sides burning with a white-hot glow.

Wilson looked down with evil pleasure as both Harcourt and Washington stared, mouths agape, at the phenomenon literally dumbfounded. "What the Hell!" Harcourt shouted.

From inside the opening appeared two stubby clawed hands, which began stretching, widening the opening. The searing hot edges of the slit did not seem to have any effect on the thick leather-like flesh covering the hideous hands as they continued expanding the opening even further. A rank odor of sulfur, human waste and decomposition filled the entire room. The hands glistened with sweat and slime, while on the end of the fingers, Showalter saw curved talon-like claws, which gleamed, reflecting the natural sunlight from the large window wall of Harcourt's executive suite.

"What in the name of Heaven!" Samuel Washington exclaimed, although he knew instantly what he was seeing appear before him had nothing whatsoever to do with Heaven.

Soon two ram-like horns forced their way through the opening followed by a mane of long greasy matted black hair. The bizarre creature, appearing literally from thin air tried to raise its head but there was not sufficient room for it to do so until it cleared the slit. Washington could see a pig-like snout dripping yellow-green snot and large tusks protruding up from the bottom jaw of its mouth, reminding him of those on a wild bore. With a great push as if the very fabric of reality was giving birth to some freakish monster, the thing rolled from the opening, landing squarely on its two huge flat feet. It stood hunched looking around the room, sniffing the air as if getting familiar with its new and uncomfortable surroundings.

The beast stood only about three feet tall, was completely naked, most definitely male by its prominent appendage, and covered from head to toe with some sort of glistening cosmic afterbirth. Its long feet had gnarled toes, with huge curved razor sharp talons extending from them. Its body, still sitting in a hunched position was a mass of sinewy muscles and brownish gray flesh covered in wet hair follicles.

Steam arose from its body indicating its core temperature was much hotter than the air-conditioned office. Massive arms, as long as its body was tall, reached easily to the floor. In its clawed hands it held what looked to be knives, but not what one would think of as typical knives, they were the types of knives one might see in a museum. They were long, curved and appeared to be razor sharp. As Wilson watched the events unfold with savage glee, a word came to his mind; 'scimitar'. He did not remember if it was a correct assessment as he was unsure if a scimitar was a type or sword or if it should be used when referring to a knife. But that was what he envisioned, a scimitar like something from some ancient civilization born of the Middle East.

The beast raised it head and gave an ear-splitting roar, spittle flying from its fang-filled maw, its slimy hair flying back and forth, splattering sweat and slime in all directions. Before Harcourt and Washington had a chance to react, the beast jumped up on the desk between them, turned toward J. P. Harcourt and proceeded to slice the man to bits. The first slash ripped across the bridge of Harcourt's nose and down his cheek, opening up a massive facial wound and sending the lower portion of his nose flying across the room. Blood sprayed everywhere. Washington now sat staring in shock, paralyzed, unable to move.

The creature continued using both of his knives to sever and slice as bits and pieces of Harcourt's body flew everywhere; a piece of an ear flying here, a sliver of lip flying there. Both the beast and Samuel Washington were completely drenched in Harcourt's blood.

After what seemed like and interminable amount of time spent savagely slicing, with one final plunge the creature shoved the blade to the hilt through Harcourt's left eye socket. The blade continued to travel up, up, through the man's brain and finally out the top of his skull. Harcourt's body convulsed one final time, then fell face first slamming against the top of the desk, driving the blade in another fraction of an inch, just enough to make a sickening wet popping sound as it exited the skull.

The horrid creature stood over Harcourt's dead carcass and grabbing its gargantuan member began to urinate on the man's head. Wherever the foul liquid came into contact with the dead man, steam arose as the liquid burned through his flesh like acid, removing the flesh right down to the bone. The creature lifted his head and howled a cry of victory, shaking the horrid thing back and forth as if in ecstatic pleasure.

The beast turned to Washington who was staring wide-eyed in terror, muttering like a mad man, his lips unable to formulate words. Washington was entirely covered in Harcourt's blood and had bits of the dead man's flesh all over him from head to toe.

The creature took his remaining knife and placed the handle in Washington's paralyzed right hand. A moment later the beast jumped down from the desk and looked up at the translucent Wilson. It gave a sly wink then dove headfirst through the opening, which slowly closed, sealing the air once again behind him.

Wilson and Showalter watched while the rip in the air closed and returned to normal, just as the office doors burst open. As the image faded from his vision, Showalter could hear women screaming and the maniacal laughter of Washington, who had clearly gone utterly insane. Showalter opened his eyes and still unable to move could see Wilson, sitting across the desk from him, still concentrating.

After a few moments, Wilson lifted his head and said "Alright, John. Here is the situation. In about five minutes, your phone is going to ring. It will be your secretary, Jennifer calling, most likely in hysterics, to tell you about what you just witnessed in Harcourt's office. That means we have very little time to conduct our business."

Wilson waved his left hand and although Showalter was still unable to move, he was able to speak and asked fearfully, "What have you done? What the Hell was that? Help..." But before he could shout a cry for help, Wilson had rendered him unable to speak once again.

"As I started to say, here is the situation, John." Wilson insisted, "I control whether or not you can speak or move. If you do what I want and you stand by our agreement, I will not harm you. If you try to fight me, you will suffer pain, the likes of which you could not imagine in your worst nightmares. I can make the horror you just witnessed in Harcourt's office seem like a picnic. Do you understand me?"

Showalter did not seem to comprehend what Wilson was trying to tell him. He did not react, just sat staring at the man. "Perhaps a little reminder might be in order." Wilson said.

Wilson tapped the phone resting near his heart and a tearing sound echoed in the office, as it had in Harcourt's office. Then in mid air, right above the top of Showalter's desk, just a few feet from his head a small rip about a foot long appeared out of nowhere. The surrounding air filled with a vile stench as the opening widened, its sides burning white hot with Hellfire. From inside the opening a long thin reptilian tentacle holding a severed human finger came forth, dropping the extremity onto this desk.

Moving his eyes slowly downward, Showalter saw the finger was his boss's, Johnson P. Harcourt. He could tell by the insignia ring, which the man treasured and never removed. The finger lay bloody on the desk top while the tentacle, complete with its small human-like hand slowly danced and waved in the air directly in front of his face. The tentacle reached around toward the back of his neck, positioning itself near his hairline an inch or so from his skin. Showalter began to sweat profusely as he felt the tremendous heat coming from the appendage. The flesh near his hairline began to redden, then bubbled as several puss filled blisters formed. Showalter's eyes watered from the pain but he was unable to cry out. Wilson could smell the man's hair and flesh burning.

Next, the tentacle pulled away back into the opening as several spider-like creatures crawled from the breach, skittering to the top of the desk, looking up at Showalter with their human-like Charles Wilson faces, and retrieved the severed finger. The things began slurping up the blood, which had spilled on the desktop then carried the finger back into the hole. The edges of the opening began to fuse back together as Showalter stared at Wilson, who sat calmly watching him.

Wilson continued, "Now, I am going to release your voice once again so we can talk but you will not shout or else I will be forced to reopen my little portal and allow my friends to have their way with you. Do you understand me John? Blink once if you understand and if you agree to follow my instructions."

Showalter blinked his eyes once and with a wave of his left hand; Wilson released the man from his inability to speak. "Please don't hurt me. I will do whatever you want." Showalter pleaded in a quiet, raspy voice.

Wilson explained, "What I want, John is what I came here for, simply to complete our deal. First, let me explain the current situation. As you know, Johnson P. Harcourt is now quite dead and Samuel F. Washington has been reduced to a drooling lunatic who will be blamed for Harcourt's murder and likely spend the rest of his miserable life in an insane asylum. Your job is now secure; in fact, I am certain this means you are about to get a major promotion. I am sure the board of directors has no one else in available as capable as yourself to fill that roll and save the company from the barrage of bad press and financial woes, it is about to receive. The bottom line is this company is now yours and no one can stand in our way, John."

Wilson reached into his briefcase and took out the contract he had prepared for Showalter's signature and laid it on top of his desk. He told

Showalter, "See? As I told you, it is still not too late. If you will be so kind as to sign my contract, you can then call and cancel your appointment with Bill Simpson and we can just go on as if none of this unpleasantness has ever happened. Oh and by the way, I won't make you sign it in blood. Ink will suffice."

He waved his hand and Showalter was able to move his right hand from below the wrist. Wilson placed a pen in Showalter's hand and put the contract within his reach.

"I would suggest signing it quickly, John," Wilson continued, "So we can begin what I hope will be a long and profitable business relationship. You see, now since you know my little secret, it means either you are with me, or you are damned. That should make the decision-making process a bit easier for you."

Showalter seemed to hesitate for a moment and Wilson inquired, "On the other hand, if you are having second thought and might prefer not to sign then maybe my little friends could pay a visit to your lovely wife, Jane or your sweet daughter Melissa."

"How do you know about them? How do you know their names? I never told you anything about my family!" Showalter said anxiously.

"I know much more than you realize, John. I make it my business to learn everything about the people with whom I do business. Jane is a beautiful woman with a great figure and beautiful milky flesh... at least for now." Wilson said in a threatening voice. "And Melissa is a pretty and innocent young teen. I would hate to think what one of those foul creatures would do with such a lovely little girl. Did you happen to notice the size of his organ?"

With out another moment of hesitation, Showalter signed the contract. Wilson stood, placing the contract in his briefcase, and waved his hand, releasing Showalter from his paralysis. Wilson reached out to shake hands with Showalter, who did not stand and sat without offering his hand. He looked at Wilson with what appeared to be equal measures of terror and revulsion.

"Very well." Wilson said, "Have it your way, John. Nonetheless, I will keep my part of the bargain. It was nice doing business with you and I look forward to our next meeting and to building a long and prosperous business relationship. And just so you know John, there definitely will be a next meeting. By the way, I will be watching you, as you know I can. If you do anything to try to sabotage the good work we did here today I will be back sooner, rather than later. Or perhaps I should say I will be sending my little friends back? You do understand, don't you John?"

Showalter nodded understanding and Wilson offered a final, "Oh yes, and congratulations on your upcoming promotion. I am sure the company will continue to grow and prosper under your leadership, and with my assistance."

Wilson turned to leave the office as Showalter's desk phone began to ring. As he walked out the door, he saw Jennifer, the secretary in tears screaming incoherently into the phone. Wilson walked by, smiling at the woman who looked up at him stopping mid sentence, staring in disbelief. As with the guard at the front desk, she thought she must have been imagining things. For a second, what she saw, or what she thought she saw was not possible. It was as if some type of demonic face was sliding around just below the surface of Wilson's outer skin, as if he wore a translucent mask not quite covering something unearthly lurking beneath.

As Wilson walked to the elevator, he saw Showalter running from his office, startling his receptionist back into reality, and then heading down the hall toward Harcourt's office. Wilson had little doubt Showalter would keep his part of their bargain. After all, Showalter had just made a great deal for his company, and it was essentially going to be his company once all dust settled from this unfortunate situation.

When Wilson entered the elevator and the doors began to close he saw the elevator doors across the hall open as several police and emergency people exited, running rapidly down the hall following the directions of the panic stricken H & W employees.

Wilson felt incredible, having completed good day's work.

## Chapter 19

As Charles Wilson was walking into the offices of Harcourt and Washington on Monday morning, his wife, Sarah, was back in Pennsylvania, on her way to the local UPS store located in a shopping center outside of the city of Yuengsville, to ship his business cell phone to his hotel.

Sarah and Charles lived on what was once a small twenty-acre farm outside of the city in a custom-built center-hall colonial home. Although Sarah liked being secluded and living away from everything, she often got frustrated when she was required to run into town for shopping trips or for emergency situations such as the one she was attempting to resolve for her forgetful husband. After settling into their cozy home, she quickly learned how 'living out' was a double-edged sword; she forfeited convenience for privacy.

One thing she did enjoy about the trip however was a three-mile stretch of road running though a wooded area thick with trees, the tops of which literally grew together across the highway, creating a canopy of shade and darkness. Even on the hottest days of summer, this section of road was generally cool enough to drive with the windows open and enjoy the fresh forest air.

On many previous occasions, while driving on the road she had opportunities to see wild squirrels, rabbits and every so often a box turtle crossing the highway. A slow shallow creek ran along the left side of the road and provided a perfect place for such animals to go for a drink. One thing she always watched out for, however were deer, which as all Pennsylvanians knew were overpopulated and abundant to the point of being hazardous. Deer often posed a serious threat to drivers on rural roads and on one occasion Sarah had struck and killed one damaging her car to the tune of about six thousand dollars. She was fortunate during that particular encounter she had not been injured.

The general rule of thumb in Pennsylvania was 'Kill the deer but don't leave the highway.' As cruel as it might sound, it was good practical advice. Much too often people would swerve to avoid hitting deer only to lose control of their vehicles, crash and end up dying themselves.

On days when it was dreary and overcast, the darkness inside the canopy of trees was such that headlights became necessary. Today was one of those headlight days. It had been raining steadily when Sarah left home and although her windshield wipers were unnecessary under the thick shelter of leaves; she did need to turn on her headlights as the dismal day plunged the covered road into an unnatural darkness.

Sometimes when she was driving this stretch of road she would pull over to the side of the road and just sit with her window down listening to the sounds of nature. She loved to hear the flow of the creek, the birds chirping and the rustling of the leaves. She had even become so relaxed on one occasion that she had actually fallen asleep in her car along the side of the road and a passing state trooper had to wake her when he stopped to see if she needed assistance. Today however, she was on a mission and did not have time to stop; Charlie needed his cell phone.

Since the rain was virtually non-existent under the canopy of trees, she was able to open her window to take in some of the wonderful scents which nature had to offer. She leaned her head out the window taking a deep breath of fresh air. To her surprise and dismay, something seemed very wrong with the scents in the air. She could not place the odor but it had a musky and feral smell like those of some wild animal. But, it was not the only thing she sensed. There was a sulfurous foul excremental stench, lingering just under the surface which she did not recognize but which made the hair on the back of her neck stand on end as some primal intuition warned of eminent danger.

She slowed down and watched both sides of the highway wary of what this strange feeling might mean. Then she saw something up ahead. Near the side of the road, her headlights caught a familiar reflection of bright animal eyes. "Deer" she said aloud, instinctively slowing down to allow for the slick surface of the highway. She had not gone much further when an enormous buck, perhaps twelve-points or more walked into the middle of roadway. She looked into her rear-view mirror to make sure no one was behind her and brought her car to a complete stop perhaps ten feet in front of the incredible beast. It stood in the middle of the road looking at her through the windshield with eyes appearing surprisingly intelligent; knowing. There was something in its look so unnatural, her arms were covered with goose flesh, as a chill descended though her body.

She was in awe of the massive size of the beast, the bottom line of his stomach perhaps a foot above the hood of her car. Its legs were long and rippling with muscles. She looked up again to see the same strange eyes staring at her, as steam billowed from the creatures flaring nostrils in the cool morning air.

She had never been this close to a wild buck before and had never seen one anywhere as incredibly huge as this beast was. It was nothing like she had ever imagined, with its giant rack of antlers seeming to sore high into he air and its thick muscular neck leading down to a massive bulging chest. At this close distance, the foul odor she had detected earlier was even stronger and made her stomach turn in disgust. She had been close to many animals before such as cows, pigs, horses and circus animals such as elephants but had never quite smelled anything as disturbing as this. She felt the reek emanating from the beast was not born of nature, but was spawned by something else, something foul and unclean. She covered her nose with her hand and quickly raised her window and turned off the air vent to try to keep the stench out of her car, but this did little to reduce its troubling effect.

She had no idea what she should do next, so she did the first thing which came to mind, she honked her car horn repeatedly with the hopes of frightening the beast into moving. The hulking creature simply stood, staring at her through the windshield, its eyes seeming to blaze brighter as if it had a simmering anger building inside, growing ever greater.

Sarah decided to try to drive around the animal; since it was a two-lane road and the buck was standing on her side with no oncoming traffic approaching from the opposite side of the road. She backed he car up and attempted to maneuver slowly past the creature. The buck again walked in front of her vehicle, blocking her ability to pass.

Now she was beginning to get nervous, it was almost as if this hulking beast had a level of intelligence much greater than should be available to its species. It seemed to be taunting her to be playing some type of game with her; challenging her. Once again, she backed up then tried to pass the creature on the right side of the road. However, before she could complete the move, the massive buck was once again standing in front of her blocking the road.

A cold terror began to overcome her as she realized she was alone on this dark section of roadway with an incredibly large and dangerous animal behaving in a completely unnatural manner. And there was no sign of any other cars in sight; no one to offer her help. It was practically mid morning and there should have been more cars on the road, but there were none as she found she was alone with the massive buck.

She considered picking up her cell phone and dialing 911 to ask for help, but then realized how foolish she would sound. She knew no emergency operator would take seriously a call from a woman claiming a large buck was blocking her roadway. In addition, when she looked at her cell phone she noticed she must have been out of cell tower range as she was receiving no signal. She had to find a way to handle this situation herself.

She thought about simply backing up and leaving the way she came but realized the next turnoff behind her was perhaps two miles back and since backing up was not her strong suit, she had no desire to attempt to back up for such a long distance unless she was left with no other alternative. Furthermore, she had to get to the store to mail Charlie's phone. She began to get angry and frustrated, deciding no stupid animal was going to get the best of her.

Once again, Sarah backed her car, further this time, and then punched the accelerator to the floor speeding toward the deer, horn blaring. Then at the last moment, she slammed the breaks and slid, skidding directly at the animal. Despite her growing anger, she did not wish to hit or kill the beast, only frighten it into moving out of her way. The beast never bolted, or showed any sign of fear; it simply stood staring as her car slid to stop just inches from its forelegs.

Furious, Sarah pounded her hands against the steering wheel repeatedly in frustration, the horn blasting in a staccato rhythm from her irritated blows. She did not know what else to do. She could not bring herself to run headlong into the buck, knowing doing so would either kill him or break his legs, not to mention the damage it might do to her car and she might also be injured. Judging by its size of the beast, the thing might collapse onto her vehicle crushing both her car as well as Sarah.

Then she had an idea. Perhaps she could nudge the buck into moving. She slowly inched her car forward, barely crawling until the front of her bumper touched the foreleg of the giant beast. She thought perhaps when the creature felt the force of the car pressing against its body it would realize it had no choice but to move. The buck did not move or flinch. Sarah looked up through the top of the windshield and saw the creature looking angrily down at her from far above. She returned his angry stare, and in utter frustration lost all thought of concern for the animal and pressed the gas pedal to the floor. The car's tires spun wildly as the car sat in place, pressing upon the muscular legs of the buck. The car's engine roared as the RPM increased, but it remained unmoving as if stuck in a pile of snow, or on a patch of ice.

Sarah could not believe the animal could be so strong, able to withstand the full force of an automobile with just its forelegs. It was simply not possible. Her car should have snapped his legs like twigs and crippled the beast, but it had no effect whatsoever. Now her frustration and fear began to grow even stronger, as she sat with her heart thumping in her chest. She had to find a way off this roadway, even if it meant backing up. Something was very wrong here. She turned in her seat preparing to back up and away from the creature.

As if sensing her decision, before Sarah had the chance to put the car into reverse, the huge beast suddenly rose up on its hind legs, putting its forelegs about twenty feet into the air. With an incredible thrust downward, the creature slammed it front legs hard onto the hood of Sarah's car, crushing it and sending a billowing cloud of steam skyward.

Sarah screamed with terror and gripped the steering wheel tightly as the car's engine shut down. She twisted the ignition key repeatedly, but the engine would not turn over. Through the rising steam, she watched the buck return to its regular standing position, still staring at her through the windshield, but now its eyes glowing blood red with a fury and fire the likes of which she had never seen before from any of natures creatures. It was then she realized this was no normal creature born of nature.

Then something inconceivable happened. The massive brute began to tremble and convulse spasmodically, as if in the throws of a seizure, looking to Sarah as if it were moving in some sort of jerky erratic alternating fashion; first blurring then coming back into focus. Sarah thought perhaps it was mad with rabies or some other disease and it might collapse at any moment. Then the beast began impossibly to transform. Sarah sat paralyzed with fear, unable to move.

The buck stood upright on its now thicker incredibly huge hind legs, Sarah was certain it would try once again to crush her car but it did not. Instead, its stood tall, its forelegs also changing, replaced by colossal arms, undulating with muscles. All four of it hooves were now gone, and in their place were lengthy hands and feet equipped with long sharp claws. Now standing in the roadway where once a buck stood was a ghastly horrifying demonic beast, well over thirty feet tall, the top of its hideous head scraping the branches, forming the canopy of leaves.

Sarah looked through the windshield above the rising steam cloud and saw the face of the creature. It appeared to be part buck and part something else, unnaturally unidentifiable. Its snout had shrunken in size becoming pig-like, and its harmless flat vegetarian teeth were now replaced with the incredibly long sharp fangs of a carnivore. The thing's antlers had risen upward and moved back on its head resembling two multi-bladed swords jutting backward from its skull. The huge raging monster beat its chest with its massive fists and roared in its fury, the sound vibrating the windows of the car and causing Sarah to cover her ears in an attempt to suppress the ear-shattering volume.

The incredible creature lifted its left leg and brought it down hard on the hood of Sarah's car, crushing it completely flat and shattering the windshield into a web of millions of tiny cracks. The back end of the car lifted at least four feet into the air and as the beast removed its foot from the hood, the back end slammed to the ground with a crash. Sarah felt as if her bones would break from the rattling impact.

Not knowing what else to do, Sarah grabbed for the door handle, swinging the passenger door open and falling out onto the roadway, scraping her legs and hands. She crawled for a few feet along the ground before struggling to her feet and running clumsily away from the scene as best as she could. She heard and felt an incredible pounding sound, the ground rattled beneath her, as behind her the beast trotted after her; each of its single lengthy steps equal to many of hers. Within seconds it was upon her.

She felt the air forced out of her lungs as the creature wrapped its huge hand around her midsection, picking her up as if she were a child's toy. She became aware of excruciating pain as the beast's claws dug into her stomach area and she felt several of her ribs crack under the creatures unimaginable pressure. She screamed in agony but her screams were cut short by lack of air as she realized one or both of her lungs had been punctured. Looking down she saw her abdomen had been ripped open by the creature's sharp claws and her entrails were falling from her body dangling like fleshy bloodied bungee cords between the fingers of the monster.

In one quick motion, the creature threw the broken woman back toward her car, where she flew through the air, at unbelievable speed over top of the vehicle, slamming into a tree on the side of the road. Her shattered body became impaled on s broken branch jutting out from the trunk, where she hung limp in position for a few seconds, before her dead body slid off, falling to the sodden ground with a sickening thud.

The giant beast bent down and using its incredible strength pushed the disabled car off the road slamming it into a tree right next to the one where Sarah had hung impaled and now laid crumpled on the ground. Making a fist, the beast slammed down on the roof of the car sending the windows exploding out in all directions.

Its work now complete, the horrid monster walked over to the side of the road next to the destroyed car and sat down. Taking one of its razor sharp talons, it cut a wide slash across its own stomach allowing blood and innards to flow freely onto the highway. Then it lay down next to the car and once again transformed back into the shape of the buck, and lay dying along the road.

Much later, a passerby would eventually come upon the scene and call for assistance. The police investigation would report the same results, as most witnesses would assume, Sarah tried to avoid hitting the buck but not only struck the beast but then lost control of her vehicle, crashing into the crop of trees. They would take for granted she must not have been wearing her seatbelt, and as a result catapulted through the shattered windshield, striking the sharp broken branch of the tree and was killed instantly.

Police would try to contact Charles at home and on his cell phone to notify him of the tragic accident, but they would not be able to reach him, because the only cell phone he had in his possession could not be reached; at least not from this world.

## Chapter 20

Leaving the offices of Harcourt and Washington, Charles Wilson walked nonchalantly down the street toward the parking lot where his rental car waited to return him to his hotel. He had another meeting later in the afternoon with a perspective client but was not concerned about the appointment at the moment. In fact, he had decided he would call the client from the hotel and cancel, fabricating some lame excuse. "Why not?" Wilson thought with a arrogance born of power, "I can do whatever I wish, whenever I wish."

He was starting to rethink his entire philosophy on life. After all, with his newfound abilities, why should he subject himself to the demeaning process of calling on perspective clients, pretending to have an actual interest in their mundane personal lives and doing anything and everything necessary to make friends with them, simply to score a sale? He realized he no longer had to do that sort of thing. Come to think about it, he no longer had to put up with working for his pain-in-the-butt company or his pain-in-the-butt boss any longer, either. If he chose to, he could simply take over the company.

Just twenty-four hours ago, he was frantically concerned about making the much-needed commission on the H &W deal as well as the promotion which might follow. Now he could care less. Suddenly the commission seemed like a pittance. The promotion seemed unimportant. Even the idea of forcibly taking over the company did not seem grand enough for him. These things may have mattered to the old Charles Wilson but the new and improved Charles Wilson had an entirely different outlook on life.

He was already reformulating a new life plan. Yes, he probably would take his commission from the H & W deal, but he would no longer be in need of the promotion. Wilson decided right then and there, he would put together a business plan for starting his own software company, a mega software company. He would hire the best and the brightest minds he could find as well as a crack sales force and would literally bury the competition, no matter how big or how grand. But he had to take some time to figure out exactly how he would accomplish this, not to mention how he might finance such an operation. He now had the power to acquire all the money he needed but he had to do it just right, without reveling how he had done so.

As he walked down the street, deep in thought, he could not help but notice the strange looks the pedestrians were casting in his direction. They all stared sideways at him as if afraid to make direct eye contact or as if they were wary and uncertain of him. Everyone seemed to step aside as he walked by.

Wilson was not comfortable at first with these reactions, remembering how he would often step aside when a homeless person or obviously deranged individual was walking down the street mumbling to himself. He wondered if he was giving off that sort of vibe right now and if it was what was causing the people to react so strangely to him. He passed one woman walking a small dog. The woman moved over out of his way, a look of uncertainty on her face. The dog looked up at him, whined once and lost control of its bladder, piddling all over its own back feet.

A half hour later Wilson walked into the lobby of his hotel, past the registration desk when he heard a voice call his name.

"Mr. Wilson?" A female voice called. Wilson looked around and saw the young girl who had originally checked him into the hotel the day before. Wilson approached the counter as the woman said uncertainly, not looking directly at him; "I have a message for you." She seemed as if she was forcing the cheery attitude toward him when perhaps she might really have wanted to be as far away from him as possible.

The girl handed Wilson a folded note, which he took and read immediately. It was from his boss, T. Martin Edmondson and read simply, "Tried to call your cell... went right to voice mail....call me ASAP about H & W."

Wilson chuckled to himself. What a difference a day makes as the old song went. Yesterday he might have rushed for the elevator and headed straight to his room where he would immediately call Mr. Edmondson. Next, he would go through an elaborate explanation of how he forgot his cell phone and how it would be arriving early tomorrow morning. But that would not be the worst of it. No sir-ree, T. Martin 'Marty boy' Edmondson would not be content to let an opportunity go unaddressed. The old fossil would insist on making Wilson endure a long lecture on the importance of being in contact at all times. And how if he intended to stay a shining star at Edmondson Systems he would have to knuckle down and take his job more seriously and keep his nose to the grind stone ..blah...blah...blah!

Today, however, things would be different; very different. Yes, he certainly would call Edmondson, but not immediately, rather he would do so when he good and damn well felt like it. He would have to remember to just shut up and let the old man run off at the mouth for a while, as Wilson knew he would, at least for now; no point in screwing up his commission. However, some day very soon, things would be a much different. One day soon, the old fart would be eating his words for supper, his last supper.

Wilson exited the elevator making his way to his hotel room and chose to put off the call to Edmondson for the time being. Wilson had matters which were more important on his mind. He was trying to figure out what might be the quickest way to get some cash to finance this future company. He was now very excited about the idea. He knew he would have to do something illegal to get the money, but it didn't bother him; he simply had to figure out what might be the fastest way to do it, and perhaps the most enjoyable.

He supposed he could put on a disguise, walk into a bank and demand the money. He could handle any resistance simply with a touch of the phone. He might have to sacrifice one or two patrons to frighten the others into submission but that seemed like a small price to pay. Then he thought about the possibility of the money being marked or perhaps serialized in some why making it impossible for him to use and decided to table the idea for a while.

He also didn't want people running around telling stories about seeing Hell-born creatures tearing victims to pieces. He needed to keep his power a secret, which meant anyone who witnessed what he could do would have to be killed, not that he had a problem with such things any longer.

Now that he had time to think more about it, he realized he probably should have killed Showalter earlier this morning. It might not be a good idea having someone alive who knew about him, but he had convinced himself with Showalter running H & W, he would have an ally, a foot in the door for future opportunities. He realized he might be mistaken and might have to think about killing Showalter after all; but for now, he figured the man was sufficiently frightened and would keep his mouth shut. Besides, who would believe such an outlandish story anyway?

Then he thought of trying to hit an armored truck. He had no doubt, his little demonic friends could easily burn their way through anything modern man could devise, such as armor plating, but again there was the chance of the money being unusable to him after the robbery. Wilson had to face the realization he simply did not understand how things such as robberies worked. Yes he saw plenty of such things depicted on television but that was acting, not reality. He had to think harder, find another way to generate some cash.

Maybe instead of thinking in terms of large quantities of cash, he needed to think in terms of small amounts. The idea of trying to rob gas stations and convenience stores and the like seemed impractical to Wilson although the potential danger and thrill factor seemed to inspire him. It definitely would take too many attempts to get the amount of cash he needed, each attempt being an additional risk of something going wrong. However somewhere deep in Charles Wilson's evolving brain he felt a charge of excitement at the idea of walking into a store and robbing it not having any idea about what the outcome might be.

He thought briefly about a different approach. What if he could find a source of illegal cash; one no one would report missing? That would be perfect. He thought about what sorts of activities would produce small amounts of illegal cash which never would be reported. Several ideas came to immediately to mind, drugs, hookers and gambling of course.

Unfortunately, theses ideas also came from his television watching habits and in reality; he again had absolutely no idea where in a town such as this, or any town for that matter, he would be able to find such activities taking place. On TV, they made it all seem so simple but the fact of the matter was Charles Wilson had always been a law-abiding citizen and had no idea whatsoever about criminal enterprises. Wilson supposed he might have to settle for finding an out of the way gas station, all night grocery, or convenience store to mark his first venture into criminal activity. After all, he had to start somewhere.

## Chapter 21

Wilson supposed he would need to rest if he were going to spend half of the night roaming around in search of cash. He also needed to cancel his afternoon appointment as well as the appointment he had scheduled for the next morning. Then he wondered what he would do if he was successful. How would he get the cash home? He might consider shipping it home but worried the money might be somehow detected, or worse, might become misplaced. He had a flight booked but probably couldn't take the money on the plane with him. How could he get it past airport security? After a few moments, he decided if he was lucky tonight and had a large amount of cash to move, he would simply cancel his flight and drive his rental car home. Why not? Yes it might take an extra two or three days to get home but he was certain he could come up with some excuse to justify his actions to his boss and his wife. He thought about Sarah briefly and was considering calling her but he was very tired and had too many plans to make and he simply forgot about calling her.

Then suddenly Wilson remembered he needed to call Edmondson. He dreaded the call but decided he might as well get it out of the way. Then old Marty boy would at least leave him alone for a while. So reluctantly, Wilson dialed his boss's number and prepared to half-listen to another ridiculous lecture from the 'wise' old man.

After a few rings, T. Martin Edmondson's annoying secretary, Betty, picked up the phone. "Good Morning, Edmonson Systems. Mr. Edmondson's office."

"Betty. This is Charlie Wilson. I had a note here at my hotel Mr. Edmondson needed to speak to me right away." Wilson said.

"Oh! How nice of you to finally call." Betty replied sarcastically. Wilson hated the old bag. Just because she was secretary to the main man did not give her the right to treat others as if she were superior to them. Charles made a mental note to have a special treat prepared for her sometime in the future, care of his demonic friends. Betty continued, "Mr. Edmondson was on the war path looking for you, Charles. Please hold for a moment and I will transfer you in immediately."

The phone click for a moment and Wilson thought to himself, "Transfer this you old bag of crap." Then he heard the annoying company prerecorded commercials indicating he had been put on hold. However, he was not on hold for very long as after only a few seconds he heard the raspy old voice of his boss T. Martin Edmondson on the line shouting, "Wilson? Where the Hell, have you been Wilson? I've been trying to reach you for the past two days. What are you doing out there Wilson. You had better not be screwing up my deal!"

Wilson took a deep breath and began his explanation about forgetting his phone and so forth. Before he had a chance either to finish his explanation, or to discuss his successful signing of the deal H & W however, Edmondson found it necessary to go into one of his droll lectures on how one should and should not conduct himself in business and the importance of being in contact at all times, just as Charles knew he would. Wilson sat on the side of the hotel bed only half-listening, making mocking masturbatory motions with his hand, smiling to himself, as if to accentuate what a jerk-off Edmondson was. He decided to let the old coot ramble for about fifteen minutes as Wilson sat eyes closed resting, completely ignoring the man.

Edmondson stopped to take a breath or to gather his thoughts when Wilson interrupted him by saying with false contrition, "I understand completely Mr. Edmondson, and promise it will never happen again. I was entirely out of line. Now would you like to know how things went at H & W?" Then he thought to himself, "Or would you rather listen to yourself have verbal diarrhea for another half hour you senile old turd?"

"Oh... yes... the deal... yes," Edmondson said sounding somewhat confused, "Please tell me how things went. I assume the deal was signed and we are now their contractor of choice."

"Most certainly," Wilson replied. "However, I found out when I got there Mr. Harcourt was thinking about going with Ultra Tech instead."

"That doesn't surprise me in the least, Wilson." Edmondson said, "J. P. Harcourt and Bill Simpson go back a long way. But I knew with all the work you put into this project you would find a way to turn things around."

"Well." Wilson continued, "The old man apparently told John Showalter he was adamant about not using us but with, shall we say, my powers of persuasion, I managed to convince Mr. Showalter to sign with us anyway. That means I just delivered a multi-million dollar deal for Edmondson Systems, probably the largest deal the company has ever seen."

"You may be right Wilson," Edmondson replied, "This deal will help our little company grow into a force to be reckoned with. We will be able to play ball with the big boys now." Charles laughed to himself at the arrogance Edmondson had. If he only knew the future Wilson was planning for him, he would not be so overconfident.

"And hopefully as Edmondson Systems grows, you will remember who helped to make it all possible." Wilson interjected, still playing the part of the dutiful employee.

Edmondson replied, "Oh yes Wilson, I will not forget. In fact, when you return I will make sure you get everything you deserve for all the work you put into this." At first Charles thought he heard a note of menace in the old man's voice and wondered if Edmondson was working on some sort of double cross. He decided to continue to play along.

"Thank you very much, Mr. Edmondson." Wilson said feigning humility. Then he thought to himself, "And you will be getting exactly what you deserve from me, you washed up old has-been."

"Mr. Edmondson. I also need to mention something. There was a tragedy at H & W this morning; a major tragedy, which will change the management structure at Harcourt & Washington." Wilson started to explain, wanting to tell how Washington had gone mad and killed Harcourt.

"Not interested," Edmondson interrupted. "I have no time for H & W's problems. Is John Showalter still on the job?"

"Ye..yes." Wilson stammered, shocked at his boss's lack of interest. Perhaps the old man was finally losing it, going senile. Wilson thought of how Edmondson had changed during the last year since recovering from his heart attack. He did not seem like himself most of the time. Charles had an image of an old Model T Ford in his mind clunking down the highway with parts falling off in all directions.

Edmondson continued to rant in the background, "As long as they pay us, nothing else matters to me." Wilson could not comprehend why the old man would not have at least a little curiosity about what happened. Then out the blue Edmondson announced. "By the way Wilson. I would prefer if you would come home early now that this deal is taken care of. I want you to change your flight to leave first thing tomorrow morning."

Wilson argued, "But, I have appointment this afternoon and another tomorrow morning with potential clients. My wife also sent my business cell phone to me overnight and it should be here by tomorrow morning around ten. Coming home tomorrow morning doesn't sound very practical to me."

"I don't recall asking you what you thought Wilson." Edmondson shouted. Wilson knew the old fart was about to put him in his place again. "Regardless of what you might think, Wilson," Edmondson continued sternly, "I need you back here as soon a possible tomorrow morning. In fact, I want you to come here directly from the airport. Don't bother stopping home. I need you here immediately. Just tell the front desk at the hotel to overnight your phone to your home address and charge it to your corporate card. It will be at your house by Wednesday morning. Now get busy. Change your flight arrangements and get back here."

"May I ask what is so important?" Wilson interjected.

Edmondson interrupted, "No you may not. I will see you as soon as you return tomorrow morning. Goodbye Wilson." And, the phone went dead.

"You miserable old senile lunatic!" Wilson shouted slamming down the phone. That old man was going to get his just deserts and very, very soon. For a moment Wilson considered reaching in and using the cell phone right that very minute. He knew the phone was powerful enough to take care of Edmondson from half way across the country; after all he had used it on that horrid child rapist the night before. But, Wilson decided instead he would just wait and bide his time. First, he wanted to get his hands on his commission check, plus he wanted to be there in person to watch his creatures from the other side, ripping Edmondson to bits, right before his very eyes. Maybe he would force Edmondson to sign a document turning over the company to him in just before the flayed the old man's flesh from his decrepit body.

Fine, Wilson thought. He didn't really want to go to his other two appointments anyway and the sooner he returned home the better as far as he was concerned. But, this did put a damper on his plans to try to get some cash tonight. He might have time for one or two quick hits but that might be all. Moreover, what did he care? He had all the time in the world to put his plan together and raise his cash. Maybe tonight he would just do a test run to see how things worked out. It was probably a good idea to try it out this far from home anyway, where no one knew him, just in case something went awry.

Wilson called the airport and managed to get a flight leaving at 7:00 am the next morning. Edmondson might not be happy, as Wilson would not get into the office until the afternoon, but screw the old fart. Wilson also called down to the front desk at the hotel and told the young girl he would be checking out Tuesday morning, but a package might be arriving for him later Tuesday morning. He instructed them to overnight it to his home and to put the charge on his credit card.

With everything completed, Wilson decided to stretch out and take a nap. He thought again about calling his wife on her cell but changed his mind. She would have to wait for a while. He needed to get some rest so he was alert to start his new and exciting career in crime.

Wilson pulled the blinds on the hotel window and put the 'Do Not Disturb' sign on the outside doorknob. He put his very special cell phone on the night table next to his bed, took off his suit and crawled into bed, pulling the covers up to his neck and getting as comfortable as possible.

He quickly fell into a deep, restful, dreamless sleep.

# Chapter 22

Wilson awoke in a fog in his dark hotel room and looked at the digital clock on the nightstand, which read 9:47. He was surprised to realize he had slept from about two in the afternoon until almost 10:00 pm. He seldom slept that long during a normal night, yet in the past thirty hours or so he had probably slept over fifteen of them.

He had been more exhausted than he realized. Apparently, his newfound abilities took a greater amount of his energy then he had expected. This was good to know, as he would have to plan his future use of the phone accordingly. He wondered if he were in his twenties instead of his forties, would using the phone exhaust him as much. Somehow, he guessed no matter what age, the sheer energy it took to release such unearthly powers would be enough to weaken anyone.

He stumbled into the bathroom and once again was shocked by the face looking back at him from the mirror. "What a mess!" Wilson exclaimed. He thought he looked as though he had been out partying all night with a heavy metal band and had taken too many unidentifiable substances, and then woke up in a fleabag motel naked with three dead hookers and a goat. He chuckled to himself at this image.

Wilson said aloud, "Wow! It looks like I need to freshen up a bit; maybe a lot." He started a hot steaming shower; his second of the day, and climbed in to revitalize himself in the hot flowing water. While enjoying the refreshing spray, Wilson started to formulate a plan for the night. He had to find some places to score a few quick hits to throw some fast cash together.

As he stood under the water's soothing massage, he started to question his motives. He wondered if he was actually planning these robberies based on the need to raise cash to start his own company, or if he was simply doing it just because he wanted to see if he could get away with it. After all, he was not in too bad of shape financially, especially with the bonus coming from his latest deal. Since his credit rating was superior, he knew he would have no trouble securing a loan to start his new endeavor. So why was he so obsessed with planning a robbery?

Just a day earlier, he never would have even considered trying to rob someone. It was a concept which never would have ever entered his thought process. He recalled for a moment how he, himself, had felt violated when the mugger tried to rob him in the alley only the night before. Now, strangely, none of it seemed to matter to Wilson any longer. With his newfound power, not only was he considering robbery, the idea actually excited him.

Perhaps it was because the strange cell phone made him feel almost invincible. He understood he was not actually indestructible, and as such, he could be hurt or killed, but he felt certain the phone could provide all the protection he might need in any situation he might encounter. In addition, maybe that slight risk factor, that possibility of being hurt was where the rush of excitement was coming from.

He became conscious of the fact this robbery had nothing what so ever to do with raising cash; maybe it truly was simply the new Charles Wilson trying to see what he could get away with; testing his power.

Regardless of the reason, Charles was eager to get out there in the night to see what would transpire. He did not plan to use the phone unless he had no other choice, especially since it seemed to drain him so thoroughly.

He already planned he would look for the right sort of business; walk into his potential victim's establishment holding the phone in his hand inside of his trench coat pocket poking the pocket out as if he were holding a gun. This way the merchant would not know whether he had a weapon or not when he demanded cash. He had seen it work on several television shows during his lifetime so he figured it must have some merit.

If the person in the store was wise or scared enough, he would simply hand the cash over and that would be then end of it. If, on the other hand the person chose to resist, Wilson could simply open up the portal release his demons and do away with the clerk. At it felt a bit odd hearing himself think in that fashion, yet somehow it also started to feel somehow right to Charles. He began to realize this ability, this power he had acquired was intoxicating and quite addicting.

Wilson knew he was a now a powerful man, a superior man; no longer a mere mortal. Any resistance to his wishes was a direct insult to his newfound power. No simple human had the right to try to stand in the way of a being who could control the very essence of Hell itself. Such defiance should and would meet with the appropriate level of retribution. Yes, Charles Wilson certainly did hope he would get to use his phone again this evening.

He walked out of the elevator into the hotel lobby a half hour later, heading directly for the front door ignoring the curious glances he received from the desk clerk as well as several guests in the lobby. He had started to become accustomed to people staring at him strangely. He had no idea why they were doing so and didn't particularly care why either. He assumed it was the new air of superiority surrounding him; the confidence he exuded.

Wilson found himself walking down the same side street where he had his encounter with the old man the previous evening. However, on this Monday night things were quite different, in that several of the local stores were open for business. Wilson passed a newspaper store, looking into the window and seeing several people lined up to buy cigarettes and play the lottery. That particular store would never do. He walked on noting the next several stores he encountered were closed.

He came upon a local pharmacy, but decided the place was too well lit for him to take the chance. He had also noticed security cameras spread throughout the store. After a few more unsatisfactory possibilities, he came to the corner where the mysterious store from last night was located. It stood empty, dark and abandoned as if no one had used it years. He cautiously peered in the window but saw nothing but blackness. The cell phone in his coat gave a slight pulse, which he seemed to feel all throughout his body. The pulsation made him feel stronger, as if he and the phone were forming some sort of symbiotic relationship, as if he was becoming one with the phone.

As Wilson stood pondering, he slowly turned to notice a dimly lit store across the alley and down the street about a half of a block. All of the businesses surrounding that one appeared closed. Wilson realized the business might very likely be the one he needed to hit.

# Chapter 23

Wilson walked slowly across the street making his way toward the business. He looked casually through the front window as he pretended to walk by noticing it was a convenience store. From a first glance, he did not see anyone inside save the cashier who was a disheveled looking muscular man about thirty-five. Wilson immediately recognized this character might not be a pushover and might give him some trouble. He chuckled to himself as he thought of how any resistance from the clerk would be met with a quick reprisal thanks to his phone. This clerk might be big and bad looking but Wilson knew the man would tremble a cry like a school-girl when confronted with the ultimate power he possessed.

As he walked through the front door, a bell above the door issued a tinny clang and Wilson was immediately reminded of the previous night when he heard a similar bell clang as he entered the strange store where everything started. For a moment, a chill ran down his spine until he remembered he was now the one with the power and he had nothing to fear. Still, the deja vu he felt upon hearing the bell's clang was very disheartening and filled Wilson with discomfort.

Charles looked about the store and saw he and the clerk were alone. The store occupied a long narrow space about thirty feet wide by about one hundred feet deep. To his immediate left as he entered through the door, he saw a service counter about twenty feet long running along the left wall. It was about five feet tall and must have been equipped with a platform since Wilson could see most of the clerk's torso above the counter. He assumed this was so whoever was on duty could get a bird's eye view of the store and be able to catch shoplifters.

Beyond the counter, shelves well stocked with merchandise extended back toward the rear of the building. On the right side of the space, shelves ran from the front of the store to the back, where they stopped at a door, which probably went upstairs to an apartment or perhaps downstairs to a basement. He wondered for a moment if anyone else might be in the building behind that door, and if such a person might try to cause him problems. He continued to examine his surroundings.

Between the two outside rows of shelving two additional rows of double-sided shelving also ran from front to back, creating three separate aisles. Wilson could see the two center rows stopped a few feet short of the back of the store allowing patrons to move from aisle to aisle while at the rear of the building. He also noticed security mirrors strategically positioned so whoever was watching the store could watch activity at the back. He saw no video cameras.

Wilson turned slowly toward the service counter and approached the clerk who was staring at him ominously.

"Somethin' in can get for you?" The man said in a gruff sounding voice.

"Yes, in fact there is." Wilson replied realizing if he was going to go through with this, there was little point in dragging things out; it was now or never. He said with much less threat in his voice than he perhaps would have liked, "If you would be so kind as to open your cash register and give me all of your cash, I promise I won't shoot you."

The clerk simply stood his ground and stared at Wilson as if he did not understand what he had just said. His muscles seemed to instinctively constrict and ripple beneath his tight fitting tee shirt. Wilson noticed the man's hair was longish, dark and disheveled and the man looked as if he were no stranger to trouble. In fact, he reminded Wilson of the type of person who might have spent the better part of his life in fights of one sort or another, a typical brawler. Wilson could not help but notice in reality the two of them should have been in opposite places, as Wilson looked more like a mild mannered store clerk while the man behind the counter looked like a criminal.

"Look, Buddy." Wilson demanded attempting to make it clear he was very serious and trying to recall dialect from one of his TV cop shows, "I'm not joking here. Either give me your damned money or you are a dead man." Wilson pulled his cell phone against the inside of his trench coat pocket trying to make it appear as if he actually did have a gun.

The clerk simply stared at Wilson with a disgusted look and said with no particular emotion, "I suppose you expect me to believe you have a gun in that pocket of yours and if I don't give you what you want you are going to blow a giant hole in me. Does that sound about right?"

Wilson stood watching the man with disbelief. "Ooooh. I am completely racked with fear." The man replied feigning terror. "There is something important you need to understand before you continue to make one of the worst mistakes of your miserable old life. You see, most of the morons who come in here and try to rob me usually walk right up to me with as much attitude as they can gather, shove a hand cannon directly into my face then scream they want the money. See, that would be the scary thing to do. And, however, although it might get my attention, it would not produce the desired results either. You see, even those types, those genuinely tough guys, those scary types, most of them don't make it out of here in one piece."

Wilson stood in shock, surprised by the reaction, not to mention the level of composure this clerk possessed. He realized he had definitely underestimated this man, a mistake apparently many others had made in the past, with less than desirable results. The clerk was slowly working his way toward the end of the platform, obviously getting ready to rush down to floor level and offer Wilson a serious lesson in physical discomfort.

Wilson grasped the phone firmly as the clerk continued, "Yeah they might manage to fire a shot or two at me and might even get lucky and nick me on occasion, Lord knows I got the scars to prove it, but eventually they leave here either on a stretcher or in a body bag. You see, my friend, I am one of those special people who likes to hurt other people. I mean; I really enjoy hurting people. It's a bit sick, I admit it, but it seems to be the way my clock is wound or something like that."

Charles understood he could be in real trouble with this man. The clerk said, "So you will have to forgive me if I don't get all worked up by you poking your finger, or cigarette lighter or whatever the Hell it is you have hidden in your pocket. You see, this ain't TV and it ain't the movies pal, this is reality. And, in reality, people like you get hurt and sometimes die, and people like me tend to be the ones who do the hurting. Why is that? I suppose it is, just because it is. So I'll tell you what I am going to do for you. I am going to give you a break tonight. The best thing I can recommend is you turn around and head back out the way you came before I really lose my temper; because when I do, and I will, then things are going to get real ugly in here, real fast."

Wilson was astounded. Now what was he to do? This guy obviously had a lot more experience than Wilson had realized. But, Wilson knew no matter how big the man was and no matter how tough the man might be, he was still no match for the threat he was facing; the threat that was the new and improved Charles Wilson. The clown had no idea what sort of forces Charles held at his command. Wilson knew this was a perfect test for his new evil friends. Chances were, most of his future encounters would be much easier than this one, so why not accept this as what it was, a great opportunity to test the waters.

Wilson pulled his right hand out of his trench coat pocket and showed it to the clerk saying, "Very well. You are correct. I do not have a gun, but I don't need a gun.... because I do have this!" With a flurry of motion, Wilson held up his ridiculous looking cell phone and prepared himself for what was to follow. The clerk looked on in bewilderment.

The huge man watched Wilson proclaim his strange declaration, unsure of what to think. From his vantage point Wilson looked like a genuine street crazy, standing there waving his bizarre looking phone about the air mumbling a variety of threats, none of which the man actually bothered to listen to, he was too busy trying to decide what to do with the loony. The clerk knew he was going to have to bust this character up a bit then throw him out of the store. He really didn't want to get the cops involved and by the looks of things he probably wouldn't have to. This guy was obviously just a harmless kook.

Wilson now knew he was actually going to enjoy this. The idiot clerk had no idea what sort of wrath he had just brought upon himself. Wilson was thinking he might make the man suffer for quite a long time before he finally allowed his pets to drag his flayed carcass into the abyss. Maybe he would have the man's guts ripped out and have him choked with his own intestines for a while as the tentacles slowly flayed his flesh away to nothing.

Wilson screamed at the man at the top of his voice. "Prepare to face the demons from the very bowels of Hell." He waved his phone about his head in a circular motion. "In a few moments you will be begging for death to end your agony but death will not come until I have enjoyed watching you suffer for a very long time. Prepare to die you insolent piece of mortal garbage."

"Look buddy." The clerk said, "I don't want to have to involve the cops in this. You seem like a harmless old coot. So why don't you just take your magic cell phone and get out of here before I have to come around and throw you out."

Wilson stopped and looked up at the man in amazement. Nothing had happened. No portal opened. No creatures came forth to do his bidding. Nothing happened. Wilson shook the phone and struck it multiple times trying to get some sort of reaction but not a single thing happened.

# Chapter 24

By the time Charles realized his phone was not working, the massive clerk had made his way to the end of the platform. While stepping down to the floor level and rounding the counter the man grabbed a large baseball bat he apparently kept hidden for just such occasions.

The smart thing for Wilson to have done at this point was to turn and run from the store as fast as his feet would carry him. But, when he saw the large man approaching with the menacing baseball bat at the ready, he panicked, shoved the useless cell phone back into his coat pocket and ran of the far right aisle of the store, back toward the rear. When he got to the door in the back of the store, he grabbed the door handle hoping for another way out but found it locked. Looking back down the aisle he saw the clerk walking slowly and menacingly toward him bringing his bat down into his open palm, showing Wilson he was about to receive the beating of his life.

Wilson rounded the corner  at the back and headed down the center aisle toward the front of the store. Half way down the aisle, he had to stop suddenly as the clerk landed directly in front of him. The agile man must have climbed the shelving and jumped over to block Wilson's escape. Charles could see there was a savage anger in the man's glare and the clerk had only one intention, to hurt Charles very badly.

"Look", Wilson said, backing up slowly, "I'm really sorry about all this.... It is just some sort of misunderstanding.... I haven't been myself lately... I am honestly sorry.. just please, let me go and I promise I will never do anything like this again... please."

The man continued to advance on Wilson, his eyes filled with anger and anticipation. He knew this man was going to beat him and maybe even kill him. And, the worst part was the hulking thug was going to enjoy it as well. As he had told Charles, he loved to hurt people, and Wilson had just given the man a legitimate and legal excuse to do what he loved best.

Wilson turned and sprinted toward the back of the store, dragging his right arm along the shelving trying to knock down as much merchandise as possible to maybe slow the man's progress. As he continued to his left and rounded the corner at the rear of the store putting him in the third aisle, he knocked down a display rack featuring glass bottles of some sort of perfume. The bottles crashed to the floor behind Wilson spilling their contents and filling the store with the overpowering smell of perfume.

The clerk was also running trying to grab Wilson, and did not have the ability to stop in time slipping on the liquid covering the floor, falling backward to the hard floor, knocking himself unconscious. Wilson slowly worked his way back into the aisle and saw the clerk lying on the floor, his clothing soaking up the perfume. Wilson looked down at the unconscious man with frustration and a substantial degree of embarrassment. This man had made a fool out of Wilson, chasing him down the aisles like a frightened schoolgirl. He had practically made Charles Wilson beg for his own life. Wilson did not understand why his cell phone had failed him but he did know this clerk, this thug was about to suffer for the humiliation he now felt.

Wilson calmly walked over to the man, bent down and picked up the baseball bat, which the man had dropped during his fall. He could have just turned and walked away. He should have just left the store. But something deep inside of Charles Wilson had changed for the worst. Something snapped; releasing a savage, primitive side of the man he, himself, didn't realize existed.

Then, letting go of every bit of fury and hatred he held inside, Wilson proceeded to bash the man's skull to a bloody pulp with the bat. When he was finished, the floor was slick with blood and brain matter and the clerk's head was no longer recognizable as human. Wilson realized now he had really crossed the line; the final line. Prior to this his actions may have caused others to kill themselves and he had used to phone to kill others but this was the first time he had ever consciously committed a brutal act of cold-blooded murder. And it felt good to Charles Wilson as if he had finally evolved, finally become what he was meant to be. He had no regrets, no remorse nothing.

Wilson saw a display with "Have-A-Hank" handkerchiefs. He took one from a pack and used it to wipe any fingerprints off the baseball bat. Then he threw the bat on the floor next to the corpse and pocketed the rest of the package. On his way toward the front door, he went around the back of the service counter, opened the cash register and helped himself to all of the bills inside. Then he calmly walked back to his hotel and up to his room as if he hadn't a care in the world.

Later in the hotel room, Wilson sat staring at the cell phone wondering why it had not worked for him. He had to figure out what had gone wrong; in order to make sure it did not happen again. Maybe he could only use it once a day. No, he knew that was not true because last evening he used it on the mugger then again in the hotel, on that child molester at the courthouse back in Yuengsville. He also had no problem with it this morning at H & W, so why now? What was the difference? The only thing Wilson could come up with was every other time he used the phone he was angry, furious at the time he grabbed on to the phone. Tonight he was not. He had simply tried to use it like a tool. Perhaps that was it. Wilson felt that had he grabbed onto the phone while he was bashing the clerks brains in, it might have worked then. One thing for certain was; he was going to have to test this phone out a lot more before he took another risk like the one he took tonight.

He found it so strange, that the fact he was now a full-fledged murder did not faze him in the least. It was as if he had completely lost his ability to feel guilt or remorse. He suspected this is how a sociopath must feel. Perhaps he was now a sociopath; perhaps he was always a sociopath. He had read an article once stating most business leaders and politicians were natural-born sociopaths. That was why they could easily close factories and fire thousands of people without remorse. He was not sure about the validity of the information, nor did he really care. He was too busy trying to figure out how things had gone so terribly wrong.

Wilson counted the money he got from the robbery and was disappointed to discover he had seized only about three hundred and seventy-three dollars. He was not sorry he had to kill someone for so little money since the clerk's behavior made the killing necessary in Wilson's mind regardless. He was however, sorry the take from the robbery could not have been more, considering he come very close to having his own brains bashed in.

Whatever the outcome, what was done, was done. Wilson decided he could not worry about it anymore. Tomorrow, he had bigger fish to fry. He was going to gather all of the anger he could when he met with his boss, the great T. Martin Edmondson. That old fart would not consider himself so great tomorrow when Wilson unleashed all of the evil Hell could offer and the old man would be screaming for mercy that would never come.

Wilson packed all of his suitcases, called down to the front desk for a seven o'clock wakeup call and crawled into bed. He had thought he would have trouble getting to sleep. He should have, considering he had just murdered a man in cold blood. His adrenalin level should have been so high sleep should never have come, but to his surprise, Wilson feel instantly into a deep and restful sleep.

## Chapter 25

Early Tuesday afternoon, promptly at 12:30 pm, Charles Wilson's plane arrived at the Philadelphia Airport after an uneventful flight. Other than the odd looks he received at the security check-in regarding his strange choice in cell phone design, everything seemed to go without a hitch; no major delays or mechanical problems.

Charles picked up his car from the multileveled-parking garage attached to the airport after retrieving his luggage. Heading westward on the Schuylkill Expressway, called the Sure-Kill Expressway by many locals, he was deep in thought, refining the plan he had started to put together while in the shower earlier that morning at the hotel. The more than two-hour commute to his office in Yuengsville would give him sufficient opportunity to work out any kinks, which might still exist in his strategy.

Wilson decided he no longer cared about T. Martin Edmondson's ridiculous little company. Although he originally thought perhaps he would force the old fart to sign the company over to him, the more he considered it, the more he realized he no longer wanted anything to do with the company. Personally, he didn't think much of the quality of personnel Edmondson Systems hired, excluding himself of course, and believed the current staff would actually become a burden to him. In addition, if the bottom line were he would have to fire everyone and start over anyway, he would rather do so from scratch with his own company and eventually drive Edmondson Systems out of business.

The old man should have turned over the reins of the company to younger men years ago but just couldn't seem to let go. And, during the past year since recovering from his heart attack the old man was acting peculiar from time to time, as if he might be losing it. Regardless, Charles knew old Marty boy would rather die than give up control of his precious little company. And, if that were the case, Charles, would be more than happy to let the old coot have his way.

Wilson had imagined many horrible scenarios, each more gruesome than the previous, depicting how he would have his demons torture the old man, and he could not wait to get started. The closer he got to home, the more the cell phone in his shirt pocket began to pulse. He now understood how the phone was able to feel the anger growing inside of him.

Wilson thought back to the robbery and subsequent murder he committed the night before. He hadn't been sure at the time why the phone had failed him, but had a strong suspicion, perhaps an intuition, it was because he had not been angry enough. He had forgotten the relic seemed to feed on anger and hatred. While in the store, he had simply pressed a button on the phone. He was now certain that was why it did not respond. Although he may have been somewhat tense at the time, he was not angry, not the kind of anger it would take to call forth the power of Hell.

Then Wilson recalled while he was busy bashing in the clerk's skull, the phone had been going absolutely crazy vibrating in his pocket. He believed had he even touched the phone at the point of his ultimate savagery, the thing might have opened a portal large enough to engulf the entire store; if not a whole city block. He still was astounded by the power the relic had and indirectly, the power he now had.

Charles also knew a lack of anger would not be a problem for him today and the phone would not fail him. He was letting his fury build greater and greater, wanting nothing better than to see T. Martin Edmondson suffer at his hand; and suffer, he most definitely would. For many years, Charles had tolerated the man's tyranny and during the past year, the old man had become almost unbearable, but now there was a new tyrant in town; and this was a tyrant with no mercy.

Just ask the clerk at the convenience store, although he would not be able to answer as his brains were currently drying on the worn linoleum floor a thousand miles away. The clerk had thought he was a street-tough, mean sort of character, but Wilson had managed to bring him down. Sure, maybe Charles had taken advantage of the man's slip up, but all was fair in love and war. More importantly, he killed the brute without the help of the phone and without a shred of remorse. He had simply bashed the man's skull in, had committed his first cold-blooded murder and he liked it; yes he like it very much. He understood he had taken a major step and had crossed over an invisible line, taking him to a new, higher level of human evolution, one from which he could never return; nor did he want to.

Charles recalled the money he had stolen from the store the previous night. He had been shocked to find there was so little in the cash register. He hadn't known what he had expected to find but three hundred and seventy-three measly dollars was a lot less than he had hoped for. He decided the small town robbery route might not be the best choice for him, exhilarating as it might be, as it would take too many small robberies to make any decent amount of money. Eventually he would put a plan together to get all the money he needed, but for now, he was determined to achieve one goal and one goal only, and that goal was to kill T. Martin Edmondson; and kill him very slowly.

At 3:00 pm, Charles pulled into his reserved parking spot outside of Edmondson Systems, frazzled from his long day of travel and seething with anger for Edmondson. He realized he had to play it cool, had to look normal, while at the same time allowing his internal anger to fester. He walked purposefully through the double glass doors and past the security guard at the front desk.

"Good afternoon Mr. Wilso.." the guard stopped in mid sentence. He was looking at Wilson with confusion and apparent discomfort. The guard was sure he must have been mistaken. In fact, he knew he had to have been mistaken. But, for a brief moment, he thought he had seen Wilson's face changing somehow. It was extremely difficult for the man to comprehend or to describe. It was as if there was a hideous 'other face' existing just under the surface of Wilson's actual face. It seemed to be swimming liquidly underneath his outer facade. In the split second when the guard believed he saw that horrible under-face he immediately thought one word, "Evil". He shook his head unconsciously to clear the image and once again saw only Wilson's outer face as Charles entered the elevator to head up to his office.

Wilson noticed the guard's startled reaction but paid it no mind, since he had been receiving a similar reaction from many people today. And, what did he care? These people were mere mortals while he was now very close to becoming a god among them. They were like ants to be crushed beneath his feet.

On the way up in the elevator, Wilson could feel the beating pulse of the phone against his heart. "Just a few more minutes." he said aloud, partially to himself and partially to the phone. "Soon you will get to have what you have been waiting for. Soon we both will have what we have been waiting for."

As Wilson stepped off the elevator, he saw T. Martin Edmondson's old bat secretary Betty signaling him from across the long expanse of the office, waving her scrawny wrinkled arms manically. She was such a maddening simple-minded hag of a woman whose sole reason for living and breathing seemed to be so she could please the old man.

If Edmondson told her to jump, she would ask "how high?" If the told her to take a crap, she would probably ask, "what color?" It was revolting to Wilson what a hopeless slave the woman appeared to be.

He had heard rumors about the two having been a hot romantic item at one time in their younger days. He assumed it might explain a lot about her behavior. Edmondson obviously felt nothing for her, if he ever did, but she appeared to still carry a torch for him. The very thought made Wilson's skin crawl.

She walked up to Wilson, apparently not noticing the hidden horrible under-face, as the guard had. Wilson thought, "The old bat is so absorbed in pleasing Edmondson she can't see past the nose on her own idiotic face. Then he decided as soon as he was finish dispatching with Edmondson, he would definitely have to take care of the old witch as well. Perhaps he would call her into the office and force her to watch Edmondson die slowly before he eventually did away with her. He thought he might enjoy watching her almighty face cave in over the horror of what she would witness."

"Charles", the woman said loudly, interrupting Wilson's train of thought, "Mr. Edmondson said you MUST go into his office IMMEDIATELY upon your return."

"Betty, please." Wilson argued trying to sound exhausted and frustrated, "I just got in from a long day of travel and would like to at least take time to go to the men's room first." In fact, he had already stopped along the way from the airport to take care of that particular bit of business and in reality couldn't wait to get in front of Edmondson, but he just enjoyed screwing with the old hag's head.

She admonished, "Absolutely NOT! Mr. Edmondson was firm about this! He said to get you as soon as you stepped off the elevator. No ifs, ands or buts."

Wilson thought to himself, "Oh, just wait, you miserable sagging sow. In a few minutes you will be licking my feet clean while begging for me to spare your miserable life. I can hardly wait to make you squirm. Maybe I will get lucky and you will become so terrified that you soil yourself. How wonderful would that be?"

"Very well." Wilson said feigning disappointment. "What Mr. Edmondson wants, Mr. Edmondson gets." He smiled slyly as he walked toward Edmondson's office knowing in a few moments, the old man would be getting a lot more than he ever imagined in his worst nightmares.

Wilson stood patiently like a good little soldier, waiting to be properly announced, while Betty called Edmondson to let him know Wilson had arrived. He heard the old fart cackling, "Send him in," over the ancient squawk box, circa 1953 that Edmondson refused to give up.

Wilson never ceased to be amazed at how such an old fashion character such as T. Martin Edmondson could be the owner of a high tech information systems company. The man didn't even own a computer! His employees may have been working on the cutting edge of technology, but the old man was part of another century.

Several years ago, during one of the old man's more mellow moments, Charles had asked Edmondson why it was he owned such a high tech company when it was obvious he had nothing but distain for modern technology. The old fool had replied he did not "give a tinkers damn" about technology, whatever that meant, and it could "all go to blazes" as far as he was concerned.

He stated he was first, and foremost; a businessman and it just happened that owning a high-tech information system was the current way he was making money. However, he did expect his employees to be on the cutting edge of developments and to be available to him round the clock, but that did not mean he had to be part of the idiotic circus himself.

Edmondson had told Wilson during his long lifetime, he had owned manufacturing companies, though he knew nothing about manufacturing. He had owned bars, restaurants, recording companies and virtually every other type of business one might imagine. And, the fact was, he didn't care one iota personally about any of them, but they all made him money; which was what it was all about to him. He said the key to success was not what you knew, but that you understood how much you didn't know, and hired the right people who actually did know. Businesses in Edmondson's mind were nothing more than a means to an end; and that end was making money. Making money was his life; his love, his passion and how he got that money did not matter.

Charles turned the knob on the door to Edmondson's office and prepared to enter, as the hatred and rage boiled ever hotter within him.

# Chapter 26

As Wilson turned the handle to enter Edmondson's office, Betty noticed for the first time the 'face under the face'. She gasped loudly and Wilson turned to look directly at her as the hideous countenance swam away, replaced by Wilson's own angry expression.

"Is something the matter, Betty?" Wilson asked, knowing full well there was, but enjoying her discomfort immensely. "Why, you look as though you've seen the devil himself." Then he chuckled, turned away and opened the door to Edmondson's office. Betty took two stumble steps backward and fell down with a thump into her desk chair, overcome with shock.

When Wilson entered the office he found Edmondson sitting behind the desk looking stern-faced and grumpy as usual, but also as if he were displeased to see Charles, rather than curious about the fact Wilson had just made the greatest deal had ever existed in the company's history.

Wilson walked deliberately into the office, closing the door behind him and took a seat across from the man, without being invited to do so, exuding an air of confidence impossible not to notice.

"Well Wilson. I would have invited you to sit down but it looks like you have already found your way." Edmondson said sarcastically. "You appear quite pleased with yourself today. I hope you are not letting your latest success go to your head. Because you know how I abhor any of my people acting too high and mighty." Charles felt his temper beginning to boil.

"Your people?" Wilson responded quietly as if contemplating the implication of what the old man had said, understanding Edmondson really did think of his workers as his people, his possessions, things he owned and he could control. Wilson knew within the next few moments everything would be changing. He felt the phone beginning to vibrate rapidly next to his heart.

"Of course, my people." Edmondson barked. "You all are my employees and I pay your salaries, quite generously, I must also say. So therefore I think of you all as my people, my underlings, my subordinates, and as I said, I prefer my people remember their places and not get too cocky. Do you understand me Wilson?"

Wilson hesitated for a moment eager to begin torturing the man, and then said as calmly as he could, "Yes, I understand exactly what you mean." The phone was pulsating wildly against his chest. It was anxious to get to work, but he wanted to delay it as long as possible to allow his loathing to build.

"You see Wilson, humility is a trait I expect from all my subordinates." The old man began to drone on as of repeating a canned speech. Wilson no longer heard what he was saying and though he was looking directly at the man and trying to appear interested, all he could hear was "blah, blah, blah, blah."

He found himself enjoying the way in which he was able to block out the old coot and think of things much more pleasant. Perhaps this was what it meant to become a type of god, as he now believed he had done. After all, when a tiger was about to rip the throat out of a gazelle, it didn't need to take the time to care about what the helpless creature was thinking. It was his victim, walking meat, nothing more, nothing less.

"Wilson?" he heard the Edmondson say to him. "Didn't you hear me Wilson? Are you all right? Or have you been struck deaf?"

"Sorry, Mr. Edmondson." Wilson said mechanically, although not actually sorry, but more out of habit than anything. "It's been a long, trying day and I must be having trouble focusing. What was it you said again?"

"I asked you to tell me about your trip and about the deal?" Edmondson said with impatience. It seemed to Wilson from his new evolved position that Edmondson really didn't want to hear about the deal any more than he wanted to tell about it, but he too was asking out of habit or job responsibility. "I want to hear how you convinced them not to go with the competition. Especially since old man, Harcourt was fuming about your forgetting your cell phone. The arrogant bastard had the nerve to call me at home; and on a Sunday, no less. It was downright heathen behavior. Doesn't he realize that is why I hire people like you? Anyway, just tell me how you managed to turn things around."

Wilson got the impression Edmondson was playing some strange sort of game with him but nonetheless gave a half-hearted explanation, trying not to let his anger seep through, "Well. I simply persuaded R. John Showalter we were the best firm for the job and he would be risking everything by going with a lesser qualified company." He was rapidly losing his patience and was like a boiling pressure cooker about to blow.

"And he was willing to take such a risk, knowing full well the president of the company was against using us?" Edmondson asked.

Wilson continued impatiently, "Look. We both know John Showalter is the real brains behind H & W's phenomenal success and growth for the past two years and those two idiots Harcourt and Washington were floundering, barely able to stay in business until Showalter came to the company. He was the one who really ran the company and he will be in control from now on."

Wilson was already getting tired of talking to Edmondson and was basically going through the debriefing process as a matter of course. But, he didn't plan on doing this little song and dance for much longer. The pressure inside of him was growing too great and he simply not hold out much longer.

Then Edmondson said something unexpected. "Tell me about this murder, about Washington going mad and butchering Harcourt right in his office. That had to be going on right while you were down the hall negotiating with Showalter. Tell me all the details."

For the first time since Wilson had entered the office, Edmondson almost looked excited at the prospect of hearing about the murder. "What kind of ghoul was this old man anyway?" Wilson wondered. Although somewhat surprised about how much Edmondson already did know, Wilson assumed the old fart must have had an inside informer at Harcourt and Washington who was feeding him information.

"You are right." Wilson said, becoming more frustrated by the minute, still having to sit and explain to the old fool, "At the same time John Showalter and I were in his office, signing the contract, Samuel F. Washington must have gone mad and murdered J. P. Harcourt in his office. We didn't find out about it until after the deal was signed."

To Wilson's surprise, Edmondson did not show any emotion what so ever, no surprise, no excitement, no shock, nothing. The man just simply sat with his hands forming a teepee, fingertips touching. It was almost as if the old man had not heard him. Wilson did not understand how Edmondson could go from being excited to almost catatonic in a matter of seconds. Maybe the old man's mind was finally giving out and shutting down. Whatever the reason, it only served to fuel Wilson's' anger to an even greater degree.

"I just told you the two owners of the company with which we just signed one of our biggest contracts in history are dead." Wilson inquired, "Don't you think maybe that is a bit shocking?"

"Ah... Yes. Shocking. Tragic." Edmondson interjected as if all of a sudden he was no longer interested. Again, Wilson got the impression the old man already knew everything about the incident. Nonetheless, this series of bizarre reactions was not what Wilson would have expected.

Edmondson said, "Then I assume R. John Showalter will be taking over the reins of the company now, at least unofficially until the board of directors appoints him president. The board will not allow something such as this unfortunate little incident stand in the way of the company's meteoric progress."

Wilson thought to himself, "Unfortunate little incident? Wow! This old bastard's heart must be colder than an ice chest full of frozen mackerel." Then he allowed this to make him even angrier, knowing it would be to his extreme pleasure to eliminate Edmondson from face of the earth. Charles decided he had had enough of this old man, this strange back and forth banter and this ridiculous staged respect for Edmondson.

"Alright, that's enough!" Wilson shouted, in a verbal explosion hurled across the desk at Edmondson, his temper rising greater by the second, as he stood up and approached the old man's desk, slapping his palm flat on the top of the desk. "I have had just about enough, and I simply can't take it any more!"

Edmondson looked somewhat shocked that Wilson would dare to speak to him in such a manner. "Wilson, what the Hell is wrong with you? Have you gone mad?"

"No I have certainly not gone mad, Marty Boy! But, I have just simply had enough! I must have been mad to put up with you and your idiotic tyrannical antics for so long. And for what? For money?" Wilson shouted, spittle flying from his lips. "Edmondson, I think its time we get something out on the table, right here and right now; time to stop this song and dance. The simple fact of the matter is I hate your miserable old rotten disgusting guts! I hate what you are doing with this company. I hate this building and every one of your worthless idiotic employees in it."

Edmondson did not say a word. Once again, he got a slightly glazed over catatonic look about him. He simply sat staring at Wilson as if he had lost his mind. Wilson ranted, "And I have changed Martin. I have changed for the best over the past several days. I have learned things about myself most men never have the chance to learn. I have learned I am a force to be reckoned with, and now you are going to have the opportunity to learn these things as well."

As his anger reached its point of climax, Wilson reached into his shirt pocket and took out the cell phone, the relic and without hesitation, pressed hard on one of the chrome skull buttons.

Behind Edmondson, the very fabric of reality began to shimmer and wave. A deep rumbling sound could be heard throughout the office as in the middle of the air, a long slit began to form from a point about eight feet above the ground. The center of the slit began to spread open as a nauseating stench filled the office. From the bottom of the slit dozens of steaming tentacles flopped out side-by-side creating a blanket of scorching writhing appendages, draping from the bottom of the portal to the floor of the office, forming a ramp of undulating flesh.

Then from the center of the slit, Wilson saw two hands emerge and begin separating the opening, widening it to allow for its exit. He was expecting to see the leathery talon-clad claws of a demon, but instead, this time the hands appeared to be normal human hands. As the slit widened Wilson was shocked to see a man stepping from the opening, and slowly walk down the carpet of tentacles, not affected in the least by the searing heat. The man appeared to be a normal human male dressed in a business suit. The man was R. John Showalter.

## Chapter 27

Wilson stood staring at the man with complete shock and confusion.

"John?" Wilson asked confused. "What the Hell is going on? What is the meaning of this?"

Edmondson sat behind his desk, watching the activities around him with no apparent interest or concern. Wilson noticed the continued incredibly off-base reactions from the man, assuming perhaps the strain of seeing the portal had been too much for him and his brain finally snapped for good.

"Good afternoon Charles." R. John Showalter said, "So good to see you once again. And thank you so much for all you have done for me over the past three days." Wilson wondered in confusion what all of this was about. Things were not working out at all as he had planned.

Showalter raised his right hand and with a jerk the strange cell phone flew from Charles Wilson's hand, hurtled across the office space to Showalter where he quickly snatched it from the air, coolly placing it into his suit coat pocket.

"My..my.. phone!" Wilson exclaimed. He had just lost possession of the one thing, which allowed him to be so much more than simply Charles Wilson; and with it went his power.

"No Charles. Sorry. My phone!" Showalter said, with a note of finality that cut Wilson to the quick.

"His phone.... His phone... His relic.... His relic." Edmondson murmured from his desk chair, watching the activities as if watching his favorite television program. Wilson was shocked to hear the word 'relic' coming from the lips of Edmondson, and in a voice seeming to be much raspier, growling and demonic. Wilson was becoming more confused by the minute and feeling a similar surrealistic sensation to that which he had felt two nights earlier at the strange store.

"What.. what is this ... all about?" Wilson stammered. "What is going on?" He was about to demand an explanation, then thought better of it and pleaded, "Please tell me what is happening."

"Yes." Showalter said. "I suppose I do owe you at least a somewhat brief explanation for what we have put you through. It only seems right. Don't you agree?" He looked over at Edmondson, who sat at his desk, patting his hands together with the excitement of a six-year-old schoolchild.

"Oh yes. Do tell John. Do tell." Edmondson said, now looking more like an aged old maniac then ever.

"You see Charles... how should I put this?" Showalter asked struggling for the right words, "It is rather complicated to explain. I needed to accomplish several, shall we say, different tasks or perhaps responsibilities would be a better term for them; and in order to do so I considered it necessary to involve you."

"One of the tasks I needed to get out of the way was to eliminate those two idiots Harcourt and Washington from the picture, and although I could have easily done so on my own, I tend to like to shall we say, 'kill two birds with one stone'. You see, my superiors also expect me to handle the job of recruiting new members for our little family. That is where you became part of the story. I have been studying you for the past year since this whole project began to take shape. And, I could tell you had what it took to be part of my team."

"Your team?" Wilson asked, perplexed.

"Yes." Showalter replied. "My team. I saw something in you perhaps you did not even see yourself; a drive, an ambition, a longing want, a desire to be much more than a mere mortal. I saw in you the lust for power, and not just the power that comes with authority or success, but ultimate power; a power such as you commanded for the last several days."

"Power. Power. Power." Edmondson repeated like a mindless robot, still sitting at his desk, bouncing in his chair excitedly and patting the top of his desk.

Showalter clarified. "In order to properly utilize you in my plan, I had to put a series of events into play. And like a great chess player, I had to be planning many moves ahead so things would work out exactly as I needed them to."

Wilson took a few steps backward and dropped clumsily into the guest chair across from Edmondson, whose idiotic maniacal grin was becoming very disturbing to him.

"Let's go back to Sunday afternoon." Showalter said. "You did not forget your cell phone on your own. You see, I am the reason you forgot it. I took over your mind for a very brief time and made you leave your phone at home. Surly, after what you have witnessed during the past several days and what you, yourself have done, you can see how easily I could accomplish this."

Wilson sat stunned, speechless, nodding his head absently. He understood things were now beginning to come together and at last were beginning to make some semblance of sense. He knew he never ever forgot his phone before. Showalter had made him do it and strangely, that made Charles at least briefly feel a bit better about himself.

Showalter continued, "I knew your flight arrangements and knew you would not be able to acquire a 'Burn Phone', as you so appropriately called it until Monday morning, so I was able to set up my little exchange at your final destination."

"But how did you know about my flight arrangements?" Wilson asked dumfounded. I arranged things through Betty and only she and Mr. Edmondson knew about them here at work. So how did you find out?"

"Arrangements. Arrangements." Edmondson said clapping agitatedly.

"All in good time, Charles. I will get to that in a bit." Showalter said. "As I said, once I got you to forget your phone, I knew you would be desperate to acquire another, as what tool in our arsenal of business weapons, is more important than our cell phones? None I would suspect. So, I arranged for one of my minions from what you refer to as 'the other side' to take the form of a helpful human stranger in the hotel lobby who was kind enough to point you down that alley to the destination I had prearranged for you."

"The strange store," Wilson said staring at nothing in particular. "with the old man."

"I have only one, and it is meant for you." Edmondson blurted out in a perfect imitation of the voice of old man in the store. Wilson looked up to see him grinning like a lunatic; drool starting to dribble down his chin. For a second, he thought he saw Edmondson's face change slightly, as if the face of the horrible old man from the antique store was swimming just under the surface of Edmondson's own face.

Showalter reprimanded Edmondson, "That's quite enough, Drabzat. We will get to your part in our little play shortly." Edmondson cringed in fear visibly shrinking down into his chair, yet still smirking wildly.

"Getting back to my account." Showalter said, "Once I got you into that alley I knew the only place you would find open was the antiquities store, because I arranged it to be that way. I suppose I could have chosen a more modern store one, which would be less strange to your sensibilities and would make you feel more at ease, but I so love making humans fell uncomfortable; I can't help myself. I take great pride in my work and take pleasure from little nuances I can insert into these life plays. I knew the condition of the store and the various works of art, which although to my particular tastes, would disturb you and throw you off your game, which they did nicely."

Showalter pointed to the humbled Edmondson. "I chose Drabzat here to play the role of the storekeeper. He had a two-part assignment, only one of which he successfully accomplished. He was to get the relic into your hands in the form of a prepaid cellular phone and was supposed to find a way to get you to murder him in cold blood. I will explain why in due time. Sadly, although he did persuade you to blow his brains out, he had to do so by reverting to his demonic form from the 'other side' and then had to threaten to kill you. Although a minor debating point technically it made your actions an act of self-defense cosmically speaking."

The creature Wilson had thought of as Edmondson, but now knew as this being Drabzat, was once again bouncing on his chair making mock motions sticking his index finger into his mouth and imitating a gun blowing his brains out shouting "Boom , Boom, Boom," then slamming himself back against his chair like a rag doll. He threw his arms over the sides of the chair, pretending to be dead, as his tongue lolled out the side of his mouth. Wilson still did not speak. This was all becoming so bizarre he hadn't a clue what to say.

"So." Showalter said, "I had to find a way to get you to understand a bit more about what the phone could do. That is why when you left the store in panic as I was destroying all evidence of its existence; you met my other minion in the alley, the 'Good Samaritan' as you put it, from the hotel lobby. I instructed him to make you feel endangered and angry so you might try to use the phone to call for assistance. I knew once you touched the phone with your anger enraged, it would demonstrate its abilities to you."

Finally, Wilson found his voice. "But that poor creature was shredded to pieces, unmercifully. His agony must have been beyond comprehension."

"Yes it most certainly was." Showalter agreed, "But to be perfectly honest with you Charles, compared to a normal day he would spend in Hell, this little excursion of pain was like a vacation for him. He volunteered for the job with pleasure."

"Well, once I got you to see what the phone could do, I needed to get you to use it on your own, to understand how your anger could power and fuel the sacred relic. But you were so terrified of the thing you would not even touch it, so I had to get you over that obstacle."

"Once again I chose Drabzat to give you a call from the other side, and to force you to answer the phone. I knew once you put the phone close to your face and felt its throbbing power you would soon stop being terrified of it and would begin to see its potential."

Wilson recalled how the old man from the store, who he now knew as the creature Drabzat, had made him feel as if his brain was going to explode until he broke down and picked up the phone. Moreover, how the voice had given him the most basic of explanations of what the phone was, almost as if to just get his curiosity moving in the direction Showalter desired.

"Then as luck would have it. You turned on the television and saw the live news report about that fine gentleman and child murder, Randal Lee Forester. It was perfect, completely by cosmic chance, but nonetheless perfect. You were so furious about the man and so drunk I just couldn't pass up the opportunity. It was just the right time for me to have you use the phone, on your own out of anger on another human being. I simply instructed the phone to buzz and present you with a basic suggestion, 'NOW' displayed on the screen and you did the rest. By the way, I want to thank you for sending Forester over to us. He has already begun his suffering and I now look extremely good in the eyes of my superiors. What an unplanned plus!"

"Next I had to begin your training, so you would know exactly what the relic was, how it worked and how you could use it to make you into a superior being. At least I needed you to believe, if I were to use you to achieve my final goals. Hence, the many events that bombarded you during your sleep. These, by the way were not simply plays meant to instruct, but were actual events and real people throughout history who have used the relic, much as you have.

Wilson recalled the various dreams he had and how when he awoke, he found his mind clear. He seemed to understand more about the phone, and had actually stopped fearing it, anxious to use it to his advantage.

"By morning, I had you exactly where I wanted you. All I needed to do now was get you into my office and convince you, your precious deal was about to go bust. I knew you now believed you were becoming some sort of god and you could control destiny. I never cease to be amazed by the never-ending bounds of human egos. So, I played my role well and eventually you took care of J. P. Harcourt and Samuel Washington for me. Did you like the way I pleaded with you to help me? I can be quite the actor when I need to be. And just for your information, Charles, I do not have a wife and daughter; they are simply more of my minions assuming their parts in the Showalter family play. However, I did like the way you threatened to harm them if I did not see things your way. It shows the promise I knew existed deep inside of you. And how did you like the way I begged you not to hurt me? Oscar nomination material, if I must say so myself."

"So with H & W out of the way and me in charge, there was just one more thing I still needed to do. I had to get you to take the final step; to actually kill someone on your own in cold blood, without the benefit of the phone. That single act was all I needed to make you a permanent part of the fold. Once again, I planted an idea in your head. It was a ridiculous idea in hind-site but you were so drunk with power you didn't even take the time to consider how idiotic it was. Really Charles, in any other set of circumstances would you have thought about robbing convenience stores and gas stations to finance a business startup? Give me a break! You made this much too easy."

"Once again you found yourself walking down my side street. But this time, I didn't have to set up a single thing. In fact, it was important I did not, because as I said, I needed you to do this on your own. I did however; disable your phone as you later found out. Again, as celestial fortune would have it, you stumbled into a store with a thuggish clerk who enjoyed inflicting pain on others. I could not have set it up better myself. The key to the final success of this operation however was all your doing, Charles. You had the chance to walk out of that store after the man slipped and was knocked unconscious. That was your chance to walk way and still keep what little remained of your tainted mortal soul in tact. But I knew you would not be able to. I knew you believed you were now above all of those things. I didn't have to do another thing but sit back and watch you commit first degree, premeditated, cold-blooded murder; making you mine for eternity."

# Chapter 28

Showalter waited a beat to allow the implication of his statement to sink in, and then spoke as he strolled around the room, "So after that, there was no need to keep you away and I decided to have Drabzat order you home."

"Drabzat?" Wilson questioned almost absently, looking over curiously at the man he had known as T. Martin Edmondson, his boss and chief executive officer of the company.

"I suppose now would be a good time to explain that situation as well." Showalter said with amusement. "Remember last year when old Marty boy's ticker went on the Fritz? Well, I am sad to report he didn't quite make it. However, by that time you and I had already begun negotiating this deal, and I couldn't let anything hold up its progress so I got my servant, Drabzat to take his place. He is quite the mimic, aren't you Drabzat?"

With that, the demonic creature occupying the body of T. Martin Edmondson sat up in his chair and started spouting admonitions in an exact imitation of Edmondson. "Wilson, I don't pay you to think. Get your sorry butt back here to

Pennsylvania right away. I need you here Wilson!"
The he sat back grinning sheepishly once again.

Wilson recalled how he had noticed the
difference in Edmondson's behavior from time to
time since his returning after the heart attack. He
was certain others noticed it as well but perhaps
chalked it up to his illness or simply old age; the
man was in his early eighties, after all. Showalter
affirmed, "Drabzat has been filling in for old Martin
for the past year. So everything you did or said,
Drabzat reported to me."

"Aye, Aye Captain!" Drabzat blurted out in
Edmondson's voice, saluting from his seat. Wilson
watched the antics of the creature, finding it so very
strange to see his boss's body going through the
motions like some zombie marionette.

"I found it very amusing how today you
returned fuming with anger intent on torturing and
killing a man that has already been dead for a year."
Showalter had to point out, "Rather funny I might
say."

Wilson sat stunned. This minion, this demon
Drabzat had taken over the body of T. Martin
Edmondson for the past year and Wilson had no
idea whatsoever. Furthermore, R. John Showalter
had wormed his way into the ranks of Harcourt &
Washington over the past two years. In Wilson's
mind, that was quite a substantial commitment of
time and took a great deal of patience.

Showalter seemed to read his mind, "I can
see you are surprised we would take so long to do
what we needed to do. One or two years may seem
like such a long time to you mortals but it is like a
millisecond to us. You see, over on the other side,
time is meaningless; it cannot be measured as it
has no beginning, no middle or no end. I can walk
back through this portal and spend the equivalent
of a thousand Earth years researching or learning
or perhaps torturing someone special for my
amusement and return right back here a minute

from now. To you, I would have been gone for a minute but in reality I might have been gone several millennia. Time has absolutely no meaning whatsoever on the other side."

Wilson was dumbfounded, trying to wrap his mind around the bizarre concepts of the temporal differences Showalter was explaining and he just couldn't quite come to grips with it. He was too logical and too much of a linear thinker to allow himself to comprehend. In his mind, everything had a beginning, a middle and an end; in that order. Even after all of the fantastic events he had been through over the past several days, this was something he could not grasp.

Charles Wilson decided now was the time to ask the final question, the one he dreaded asking, sensing he might already know the answer, "So who are you? What manner of being are you that you can control the very fabric of time and space and powers of Hell itself."

"Why, that's quite simple Charles." The man replied, "I am R. John Showalter, president and CEO of Harcourt & Wilson, soon to be known as Showalter Unlimited, in honor of the unlimited power I possess and will use to further both my corporate, personal and satanic goals."

Charles asked cautiously, "But you are much more than that aren't you John? You are the dark one, himself; Satan, aren't you?"

Showalter laughed heartily. "Me? Satan? Don't be foolish Charles. I am so far down the pecking order in Hell from the big man, that in the millions and millions of years I have served the other side, I have never even seen him once. No Charles, I am just another cog in the wheel, a minion like every other minion; perhaps a little bit higher up on the food chain than most, but not nearly as far along as others. There are millions of us out here in your world Charles walking among you in all walks of life; common people, working people, politicians, teachers, business leaders, and even people you consider icons in your religious communities. We are everywhere. I told you I have superiors. I have to answer to someone just like you and everyone else. You know the expression 'everyone has a boss'? Well, that phrase is true, even in Hell."

"So then I am no longer the keeper of the phone." Wilson said with sadness, accepting his lost power. "You are the true keeper of the relic."

"For now, Charles." Showalter said, "But eventually you will find yourself in possession of the relic again I am certain. See Charles, I told you I have many tasks and responsibilities including recruitment. That was one of the main objectives of this exercise, recruitment. I just knew you would be perfect for the job but I needed you to prove yourself, which you did. You committed a heartless, cold-blooded murder of an unconscious, defenseless man. It is hard to find something much more worthy of damnation than that. So congratulations, you have won you place in Hell, for eternity."

"So now what?" Wilson asked, not really wanting to know the answer, but still understanding he needed to know.

"Well." Showalter said, "In about five minutes or so from now you are going to assume control of Edmondson Systems as the owner and CEO. And you will lead its soon to be amazing growth."

"What?" Charles exclaimed in surprise, standing once again. He had assumed perhaps he was going to be killed. "You've got to be kidding me! That is amazing! You mean I am taking over this company?" Wilson's business sense told him although he wanted much more, now would be a good time to show some good old fashion humility. "John. I am more than honored to have you offer me this opportunity, Thank you so very much."

Then Wilson remembered his wife Sarah. "Sarah! I have to call my wife Sarah and tell her. She will be thrilled with the news."

"Sorry Charles. No point in calling her, she's dead." Showalter said.

Wilson felt as if a tire iron had struck him square in the chest. "What? What did you say?"

"Your wife, Sarah. She's dead. I had one of my creatures kill her this morning. Messy little scene it was." Once again, Charles sat down in his chair with a thump. He looked across the desk at Edmondson / Drabzat who was making a throat slitting sign across his own neck.

Within a few seconds, Wilson's mind was filled with the images of his wife traveling down the road to mail his phone and he was shown every detail of the horrible fear and subsequent pain she suffered before the beast finally killed her. Tears flowed from his eyes as he trembled, wishing his own heart would stop so he could lie down and die.

"Oh Charles." Showalter said, "Don't take it so badly. It was something, which had to be done. People like you and I must be free of the trappings of life such as wives and families. We need to be able to move through worlds unencumbered. You will thank me for this someday I am sure, but it will be a bit tough for a while. I understand that. But if it makes things any better, I should point out that there will be plenty of luscious minions for you eventually who can take whatever form you choose for your earthly pleasures, but to be honest, eventually they will not satisfy you as much as the lust for power."

"Sarah. My poor Sarah." Wilson moaned, realizing he had just been handed the greatest opportunity of his business life; one at the pinnacle of professional achievement, while simultaneously losing the most important thing in his life, his one true love. As if a hole had opened up inside of him, Wilson felt as if the very essence of what made him who he really was, flowed out of him, leaving him a hollow, dead empty shell. If this were the tradeoff, then he had just made the worst deal of his miserable life.

"Alright Charles, lets get on with this. There is no reason to waste time with such nonsense as mourning. There's too much work to be done." Showalter said. Wilson sat deep in his chair as if the seat cushion itself were pulling him inside. He stared at Showalter not knowing what might happen to him next and no longer caring.

"Here is how this is going to work, Charles. In exactly five minutes, you will be taking control of this company and we will begin transforming Edmondson Systems into one of the largest Information Systems companies in the world. In less than five years you will have offices all around the world, and you will be in control of everything."

"But, but.." Charles stammered despondently, "Sarah, You.. ki..ki..killed Sarah, you bastard! I... I.. can't... I ... don't care... I ...won't."

"Not a problem, Charles old boy. As I said, you will be as good as new in five minutes."

Wilson's face filled with a rage greater than any he had ever felt in his entire life. He stood in front of his chair, hands clenched at his sides and started slowly walking deliberately toward, R. John Showalter.

"Uh oh!" Drabzat said from inside of Edmondson's body. "This isn't going to be very pretty."

"Oh yes, Charles." Showalter said nonchalantly, as if not even paying attention to the large looming figure of Charles Wilson, approaching him with obvious violent intent. He waved his hand casually and Charles froze in his tracks, unable to move.

"There is one small thing I forgot to mention. Do you recall how I said time over on the other side is completely irrelevant to time over here? Well, I forgot to mention we have a 'best practice' procedure over on the other side for developing our future leaders and subordinates. As with your various branches of military service, we find it very effective to take our candidates and break them down. In essence, destroy their ego completely so we can then start rebuilding them into the entities we need and want them to be."

With that, several long fleshy whipping tentacles flew from the steaming portal, wrapping around the lower part of Charles Wilson's legs. He felt the flesh boiling beneath their grasp, melting and dripping like tallow from his ankles as the horrid tendrils burned through to his bones. He moaned in agony unable to let out a scream then collapsed to his knees.

"You see Charles. Before you can properly learn to make others suffer, you need to learn about all the different ways Hell has to make you suffer yourself."

Another long thin feeler shot out of the opening and wrapped itself around Wilson's right wrist, pulling him closer to the opening.

Drabzat sat quietly now in his Edmondson form, shaking his head side to side as if in commiseration, aware of what was in store for Wilson.

"And the sort of important lessons you will need to learn are going to take much, much suffering and will also take a very, very long time; perhaps the equivalent of thousands of earth years."

A final limb shot out and wrapped itself tightly around Wilson's neck as the flesh of his throat began to bubble and blister. Hundreds of spider-like creature with human faces resembling John Showalter began to skitter down the carpet of undulating tentacles making their way to Wilson's body, where they began to slowly, and methodically devour him as he was dragged ever closer to the opening.

"So, as I said earlier. In about five minutes you will return to take your rightful place as leader of this company, but in the meantime there is a millennium of suffering for you to experience and learn."

All of the remaining tentacles converged on Wilson as one, encircling him, dragging him howling into the Hell fire and blackness of the abyss.

## Chapter 29

Charles Wilson sat silently, unmoving, his eyes closed tightly. As was true of the countless times before, he was terrified to open them to discover what new horror, what new torture, what new pain might be waiting for him. He had lost track of how many times he had suffered and died over, and over, and over again; each time being reborn, only to once again undergo a more violent, more horrible and more unimaginable death then the last. In his wildest of imaginings, he had never fathomed the depth of revulsion and misery existing on the other side.

Charles had stopped counting after the first several hundred times his body was battered, ripped to bits, his flesh systematically flayed and devoured while he suffered helplessly in complete physical awareness, each of his thousands of nerve ending exposed and vulnerable to the agonizing molestations. He suspected the torments he suffered had lasted for what would be the equivalent of several thousand of Earth's years. He had no true idea how long it had gone on, since there was no measurable meaning of 'time' in Hell. Likewise, he did not know how long it would continue. He was beyond wondering, beyond caring, he was simply enduring; not like he had any alternative.

Moreover, he was forced to remember every single detail, every nuance, of every moment of every torturous event. Although some might have been considered much 'worse' than others, if such a comparison could actually exist; the 'best' or 'lesser' of these horrors were far worse than what he could have every possibly imagined; whereas, the worst of them were by far, beyond the intellectual understanding of any living human.

Among the most ghastly, was one particular scenario, which Charles was forced to repeat, against his will, many thousand times. In this setting, he was forced to take the place of the demonic creature that had killed his beloved Sarah. Permanently burned into Wilson's consciousness were the details of the thousands of times he had not only watched his sweet Sarah die, but had to actually be the creature killing her. He recalled the terror in her eyes, and the agony she felt as he had to rip her to pieces and throw her broken body through the air, impaling her on that accursed tree branch. Wilson would have gladly volunteered to have his flesh torn from his body a million times rather than have to endure the anguish of being forced to kill his Sarah yet again.

There was a time when he thought he might not be able to take any more of the suffering, and might just shut down; but doing so was never an option. There was no giving up, no shutting down because after every unimaginable death there was complete rebirth; there was always the next time with more pain, more anguish, more torture; never ending agony over and over and over and over again and again. Charles learned his lessons well and learned exactly what the word 'eternity' really meant.

So here he was once again; waiting to open his eyes, waiting to see what horror was in store for him this time. What unimaginable little corner of Hell he would find him self in; what tortures he would have to endure next, and for how long. What new form of evil would be forced upon him this time, what demeaning sexual act, what inconceivable indignity? He knew there was no limit to what he could be made to suffer, because he had reached and passed his limit many thousands of times over and yet there would always be more.

As he sat, eyes closed, he tried to take in the scents of his surroundings. It seemed somewhat familiar to Charles, not unpleasant on the surface but underneath, he could detect some foul aroma he recalled from his childhood and yes, he recalled the odor again from that strange store where he first come in contact with the relic, the phone, thousands of lifetimes ago. That stench of death, old age and decay, which had surrounded the old man in the store; the man Charles later learned had been the demon Drabzat. That foul reek, he had recalled from his own childhood clinging around his dying grandfather, now seemed to exist nearby as if taunting him once again.

Charles tried to move and noticed he was not able to do so. He seemed to be paralyzed, but nonetheless was not frightened or concerned. Compared to what he had been through during his time in Hell, a little paralysis might be considered a welcome relief. After all, paralyzed people could not feel things, and he certainly did not want to be able to feel a thing if he were going to experience yet another agonizing situation.

"Charles? Are you in there?" Wilson heard a voice; a familiar voice he recalled from the past, but in his confusion could not quite place. It was a voice from what seemed like several millennia ago. Then a face began to swim into his memory to accompany the voice, followed soon by a name as recognition took shape. The voice he heard was that of the creature who had sent him into Hell; the voice of the man, R. John Showalter.

Wilson slowly opened his eyes and found he was back in the office of T. Martin Edmondson, CEO of Edmondson Systems. He still could not move, but nonetheless was happy to know he was no longer on the other side. He could hear distant moaning, indicating the portal to Hell was likely open somewhere behind him. He thought he could hear the frantic whipping of the tentacles and the skittering of the spider-like things. He could smell the sulfurous odor coming from the opening and could feel the heat radiating against his back.

He forced his eyes downward to look at the desk calendar and noticed by the date, and the time on the desk clock, it was still the morning of his eventful return to Pennsylvania, and only a few minutes had passed. He recalled Showalter telling him about the temporal difference between earth time and time in Hell. Although he had been away for thousands of years of pain and torment, he was now right back in Edmondson's office, just a few minutes from when he left. He could still not comprehend how he could have suffered and died thousands of thousands of times over, yet it was only now a few moments later then when he left to begin his 'training'. He looked straight ahead and his eyes met those of R. John Showalter.

"Welcome back Charles. I hope your stay was a pleasant one." Showalter said, knowing full well exactly what sort of stay Wilson had experienced. "I hope your training was everything you expected and more. I feel like I haven't see you in a thousand years." He laughed knowingly.

"Now that you have been properly indoctrinated into our little fold and you have gotten to see just how bad, bad can be, I think it is time we get back to the business of building this company. I have taken the liberty of immobilizing you for a little while until your body acclimates itself back into the environment in which you currently reside. Plus I have some issues to take care of that should be making themselves known right about.......now."

Without delay, the squawk box on the top of Edmondson's desk gave a squeal then Wilson heard Edmondson's secretary Betty say. "Mr. Edmondson, sorry for breaking in on your meeting but I have a very important call for Charles from the Pennsylvania State Police. They want to speak to him immediately." Charles was not sure what was going on at first, and then remembered his wife, Sarah's death had occurred that very morning.

Showalter pressed the 'talk' button on the squawk box and said in a perfect imitation of T. Martin Edmondson, "Thanks Betty, dear. Will you be so kind as to transfer the call in to my phone?" Wilson could imagine Betty gushing over hearing the term 'dear' in Edmondson's voice. If she only knew the old man she was in love with had been a walking zombie for the past year.

Next Showalter answered the phone in Wilson's voice. "Charles Wilson speaking, how may I help you?" Showalter sat with the phone at his ear then in a panicky grief filled voice he shouted, "What?... Are you certain....Oh my God no! Not Sarah!..." Then he issued a garbled noise sounding as if he were in physical distress and hung up the phone. With a wave of his arm, Showalter freed Wilson from his paralysis while explaining the final part of his strategy.

"I am going to be leaving you now Charles. However, as I said, I want you to take your place in command of this company immediately. I will be back in contact with you shortly with further instructions. Remember your time on the other side and remember I will be watching. Any attempt by you to do other than what I require will result in another special orientation session, if you get my meaning." Showalter stood and strolled across the room, walking up into the still open portal to Hell and disappeared as the opening closed behind him.

Wilson did not know what to do. He was still not completely oriented to his surroundings and was a bit confused. His muscles ached and he felt as if his bones were racked with pain as well. And there was the awful smell again; aged, foul, decaying.

Suddenly the door to the office burst open and Betty followed by several office workers raced inside. "Oh My heavens no!" Betty cried. "Poor Charles. That poor man! The strain of learning about Sarah must have been too much for him."

Wilson looked at the woman as if she had lost her mind. What was she talking about? He was sitting right in front of her looking directly at her. Then he looked down on the floor next to the front of the desk and saw his own body laying prone on the floor, his skin ashen, and his lips blue. His hands appeared to be gnarled in a claw-like shape clutching at his chest. Charles could not understand what was happening. How could he be lying dead on the floor yet standing looking over the desk at his own dead body?

"Oh. Mr. Edmondson. This is so tragic!" Betty said rushing toward Wilson, hugging him tightly with her withered scrawny arms and pressing her sagging breasts against his chest and her bony nose into the crook of his neck." Wilson could feel Betty's tears against the side of his face.

Then he understood it all. As Showalter had promised, he was now the owner and CEO of Edmondson Systems. However, he now resided in the dead moldering body of T. Martin Edmondson. Somewhere deep in the darkest depths of Charles Wilson's mind he cried a scream of anguish for the many mistakes he had made, knowing his eternity of suffering had just begun.

6345413R0

Made in the USA
Charleston, SC
14 October 2010